The Mezzanine

Nicholson Baker was born in 1957. He has written three other novels, *Room Temperature*, *Vox* and *The Fermata*. He is also the author of a non-fiction book, *U and I*, and a book of essays, *The Size of Thoughts*. He lives in California.

Also by Nicholson Baker

Room Temperature

U and I

Vox

The Fermata

The Size of Thoughts

NICHOLSON BAKER

The Mezzanine

Granta Books
London

Granta Publications, 2/3 Hanover Yard, London N1 8BE

First published in the USA by Weidenfeld & Nicolson 1988
First published in Great Britain by Granta Books 1989
This edition published by Granta Books 1998

Portions of this novel, in somewhat different form,
first appeared in the *New Yorker*.

A CIP catalogue record for this book is available
from the British Library.

3 5 7 9 10 8 6 4

Printed and bound in Great Britain
by Mackays of Chatham PLC

For Margaret

THE MEZZANINE

Chapter One

AT ALMOST ONE O'CLOCK I entered the lobby of the building where I worked and turned toward the escalators, carrying a black Penguin paperback and a small white CVS bag, its receipt stapled over the top. The escalators rose toward the mezzanine, where my office was. They were the free-standing kind: a pair of integral signs swooping upward between the two floors they served without struts or piers to bear any intermediate weight. On sunny days like this one, a temporary, steeper escalator of daylight, formed by intersections of the lobby's towering volumes of marble and glass, met the real escalators just above their middle point, spreading into a needly area of shine where it fell against their brushed-steel side-panels, and adding long glossy highlights to each of the black rubber handrails which wavered slightly as the handrails slid on their tracks, like the radians of black luster that ride the undulating outer edge of an LP.[1]

When I drew close to the up escalator, I involuntarily transferred my paperback and CVS bag to my left hand, so that I

[1] I love the constancy of shine on the edges of moving objects. Even propellers or desk fans will glint steadily in certain places in the grayness of their rotation; the curve of each fan blade picks up the light for an instant on its circuit and then hands it off to its successor.

could take the handrail with my right, according to habit. The bag made a little paper-rattling sound, and when I looked down at it, I discovered that I was unable for a second to remember what was inside, my recollection snagged on the stapled receipt. But of course that was one of the principal reasons you needed little bags, I thought: they kept your purchases private, while signaling to the world that you led a busy, rich life, full of pressing errands run. Earlier that lunch hour, I had visited a Papa Gino's, a chain I rarely ate at, to buy a half-pint of milk to go along with a cookie I had bought unexpectedly from a failing franchise, attracted by the notion of spending a few minutes in the plaza in front of my building eating a dessert I should have outgrown and reading my paperback. I paid for the carton of milk, and then the girl (her name tag said "Donna") hesitated, sensing that some component of the transaction was missing: she said, "Do you want a straw?" I hesitated in turn—did I? My interest in straws for drinking anything besides milkshakes had fallen off some years before, probably peaking out the year that all the major straw vendors switched from paper to plastic straws, and we entered that uncomfortable era of the floating straw;[1]

[1] I stared in disbelief the first time a straw rose up from my can of soda and hung out over the table, barely arrested by burrs in the underside of the metal opening. I was holding a slice of pizza in one hand, folded in a three-finger grip so that it wouldn't flop and pour cheese-grease on the paper plate, and a paperback in a similar grip in the other hand—what was I supposed to do? The whole point of straws, I had thought, was that you did not have to set down the slice of pizza to suck a dose of Coke while reading a paperback. I soon found, as many have, that there was a way to drink no-handed with these new floating straws: you had to bend low to the table and grasp the almost horizontal straw with your lips, steering it back down into the can every time you wanted a sip, while straining your eyes to keep them trained on the line of the page you were reading. How could the straw engineers have made so elementary a mistake, designing a straw that weighed less than the sugar-water in which it was intended to stand? Madness! But later, when I gave the subject more thought, I decided that, though the straw engineers were probably blameworthy for failing to foresee the straw's buoyancy, the problem was more complex than I had first imagined. As I reconstruct that moment of history, circa 1970 or so, what happened was that the plastic material used in place of paper was in fact heavier than Coke—their equations were absolutely correct, the early manufacturing runs looked good, and though the water-to-plastic weight ratio was a little tight, they went ahead. What they had forgotten to take into account, perhaps, was that the bubbles of carbonation attach themselves to invisible

although I did still like plastic elbow straws, whose pleated necks resisted bending in a way that was very similar to the tiny seizeups your finger joints will undergo if you hold them in the same position for a little while.[1]

So when Donna asked if I would like a straw to accompany my half-pint of milk, I smiled at her and said, "No thanks. But maybe I'd like a little bag." She said, "Oh! Sorry," and hur-

---

asperities on the straw's surface, and are even possibly generated by turbulence at the leading edge of the straw as you plunge it in the drink; thus clad with bubbles, the once marginally heavier straw reascends until its remaining submerged surface area lacks the bubbles to lift it further. Though the earlier paper straw, with its spiral seam, was much rougher than plastic, and more likely to attract bubbles, it was porous: it soaked up a little of the Coke as ballast and stayed put. All right—an oversight; why wasn't it corrected? A different recipe for the plastic, a thicker straw? Surely the huge buyers, the fast-food companies, wouldn't have tolerated straws beaching themselves in their restaurants for more than six months or so. They must have had whole departments dedicated to exacting concessions from Sweetheart and Marcal. But the fast-food places were adjusting to a novelty of their own at about the same time: they were putting slosh caps on every soft drink they served, to go *or* for the dining room, which cut down on spillage, and the slosh caps had a little cross in the middle, which had been the source of some unhappiness in the age of paper straws, because the cross was often so tight that the paper straw would crumple when you tried to push it through. The straw men at the fast-food corporations had had a choice: either we (a) make the crossed slits easier to pierce so that the paper straws aren't crumpled, or we (b) abandon paper outright, and make the slits even *tighter,* so that (1) any tendency to float is completely negated and (2) the seal between the straw and the crossed slits is so tight that almost no soda will well out, stain car seats and clothing, and cause frustration. And (b) was the ideal solution for them, even leaving aside the attractive price that the straw manufacturers were offering as they switched their plant over from paper-spiraling equipment to high-speed extrusion machines—so they adopted it, not thinking that their decision had important consequences for all restaurants and pizza places (especially) that served cans of soda. Suddenly the paper-goods distributor was offering the small restaurants floating plastic straws and only floating plastic straws, and was saying that this was the way all the big chains were going; and the smaller sub shops did no independent testing using cans of soda instead of cups with crossed-slit slosh caps. In this way the quality of life, through nobody's fault, went down an eighth of a notch, until just last year, I think, when one day I noticed that a plastic straw, made of some subtler polymer, with a colored stripe in it, stood anchored to the bottom of my can!

[1] When I was little I had thought a fair amount about the finger-joint effect; I assumed that when you softly crunched over those temporary barriers you were leveling actual "cell walls" that the joint had built to define what it believed from your motionlessness was going to be the final, stable geography for that microscopic region.

riedly reached under the counter for it, touchingly flustered, thinking she had goofed. She was quite new; you could tell by the way she opened the bag: three anemone splayings of her fingers inside it, the slowest way. I thanked her and left, and then I began to wonder: Why had I requested a bag to hold a simple half-pint of milk? It wasn't simply out of some abstract need for propriety, a wish to shield the nature of my purchase from the public eye—although this was often a powerful motive, and not to be ridiculed. Small mom and pop shopkeepers, who understood these things, instinctively shrouded whatever solo item you bought—a box of pasta shells, a quart of milk, a pan of Jiffy Pop, a loaf of bread—in a bag: food meant to be eaten indoors, they felt, should be seen only indoors. But even after ringing up things like cigarettes or ice cream bars, obviously meant for ambulatory consumption, they often prompted, "Little bag?" "Small bag?" "Little bag for that?" Bagging evidently was used to mark the exact point at which title to the ice cream bar passed to the buyer. When I was in high school I used to unsettle these proprietors, as they automatically reached for a bag for my quart of milk, by raising a palm and saying officiously, "I don't need a bag, thanks." I would leave holding the quart coolly in one hand, as if it were a big reference book I had to consult so often that it bored me.

Why had I intentionally snubbed their convention, when I had loved bags since I was very little and had learned how to refold the large thick ones from the supermarket by pulling the creases taut and then tapping along the infolding center of each side until the bag began to hunch forward on itself, as if wounded, until it lay flat again? I might have defended my snub at the time by saying something about unnecessary waste, landfills, etc. But the real reason was that by then I had become a steady consumer of magazines featuring color shots of naked women, which I bought for the most part not at the mom-and-pop stores but at the newer and more anonymous convenience stores, distributing my purchases among several in the area. And at these stores, the guy at the register would sometimes cruelly, mock-innocently warp the "Little bag?" convention by asking, "You need a bag for that?"—forcing me either to concede this need with a nod, or to be tough and say no and roll up the unbagged nude magazine and clamp it in my bicycle rack so that only the giveaway cigarette ad on the back cover showed—"Carlton Is Lowest."[1]

Hence the fact that I often said no to a bag for a quart of milk at the mom-and-pop store during that period was a way of demonstrating to anyone who might have been following my movements that at least at that moment, exiting that store, I had nothing to hide; that I did make typical, vice-free family purchases from time to time. And now I was asking for a little bag for my half-pint of milk from Donna in order, finally, to clean away the bewilderment I had caused those moms and pops, to submit happily to the convention, even to pass it on to someone who had not yet quite learned it at Papa Gino's.

But there was a simpler, less anthropological reason I had specifically asked Donna for the bag, a reason I hadn't quite isolated in that first moment of analysis on the sidewalk afterward, but which I now perceived, walking toward the escalator to the mezzanine and looking at the stapled CVS bag I had just transferred from one hand to the other. It seemed that I always liked to have one hand free when I was walking, even when I had several things to carry: I liked to be able to slap my hand fondly down on the top of a green mailmen-only mailbox, or bounce my fist lightly against the steel support for the

[1] For several years it was inconceivable to buy one of those periodicals when a girl was behind the counter; but once, boldly, I tried it—I looked directly at her mascara and asked for a *Penthouse,* even though I preferred the less pretentious *Oui* or *Club,* saying it so softly however that she heard "Powerhouse" and cheerfully pointed out the candy bar until I repeated the name. Breaking all eye contact, she placed the document on the counter between us—it was back when they still showed nipples on their covers—and rang it up along with the small container of Woolite I was buying to divert attention: she was embarrassed and brisk and possibly faintly excited, and she slipped the magazine in a bag without asking whether I "needed" one or not. That afternoon I expanded her brief embarrassment into a helpful vignette in which I became a steady once-a-week buyer of men's magazines from her, always on Tuesday morning, until my very ding-dong entrance into the 7-Eleven was charged with trembly confusion for both of us, and I began finding little handwritten notes placed in the most widespread pages of the magazine when I got home that said, "Hi!—the Cashier," and "Last night I posed sort of like this in front of my mirror in my room—the Cashier," and "Sometimes I look at these pictures and think of you looking at them—the Cashier." Turnover is always a problem at those stores, and she had quit the next time I went in.

traffic lights, both because the pleasure of touching these cold, dusty surfaces with the springy muscle on the side of my palm was intrinsically good, and because I liked other people to see me as a guy in a tie yet carefree and casual enough to be doing what kids do when they drag a stick over the black uprights of a cast-iron fence. I especially liked doing one thing: I liked walking past a parking meter so close that it seemed as if my hand would slam into it, and at the last minute lifting my arm out just enough so that the meter passed underneath my armpit. All of these actions depended on a free hand; and at Papa Gino's I already was holding the Penguin paperback, the CVS bag, and the cookie bag. It might have been possible to hold the blocky shape of the half-pint of milk against the paperback, and the tops of the slim cookie bag and the CVS bag against the other side of the paperback, in order to keep one hand free, but my fingers would have had to maintain this awkward grasp, building cell walls in earnest, for several blocks until I got to my building. A bag for the milk allowed for a more graceful solution: I could scroll the tops of the cookie bag, the CVS bag, and the milk bag *as one* into my curled fingers, as if I were taking a small child on a walk. (A straw poking out of the top of the milk bag would have interfered with this scrolling—lucky I had refused it!) Then I could slide the paperback into the space between the scroll of bag paper and my palm. And this is what I had in fact done. At first the Papa Gino's bag was stiff, but very soon my walking softened the paper a little, although I never got it to the state of utter silence and flannel softness that a bag will attain when you carry it around all day, its hand-held curl so finely wrinkled and formed to your fingers by the time you get home that you hesitate to unroll it.

It was only just now, near the base of the escalator, as I watched my left hand automatically take hold of the paperback and the CVS bag together, that I consolidated the tiny understanding I had almost had fifteen minutes before. Then it had not been tagged as knowledge to be held for later retrieval, and I would have forgotten it completely had it not been for the sight of the CVS bag, similar enough to the milk-carton bag to trigger vibratiuncles of comparison. Under microscopy, even insignificant perceptions like this one are almost always revealed to be more incremental than you later are tempted to present them as being. It would have been less cumbersome, in the account I am giving here of a specific lunch hour several years ago, to have pretended that the bag thought had come to me complete and "all at once" at the foot of the up escalator, but the truth was that it was only the latest in a fairly long sequence of partially forgotten, inarticulable experiences, finally now reaching a point that I paid attention to it for the first time.

In the stapled CVS bag was a pair of new shoelaces.

Chapter Two

MY LEFT SHOELACE had snapped just before lunch. At some earlier point in the morning, my left shoe had become untied, and as I had sat at my desk working on a memo, my foot had sensed its potential freedom and slipped out of the sauna of black cordovan to soothe itself with rhythmic movements over an area of wall-to-wall carpeting under my desk, which, unlike the tamped-down areas of public traffic, was still almost as soft and fibrous as it had been when first installed. Only under the desks and in the little-used conference rooms was the pile still plush enough to hold the beautiful Ms and Vs the night crew left as strokes of their vacuum cleaners' wands made swaths of dustless tufting lean in directions that alternately absorbed and reflected the light. The nearly universal carpeting of offices must have come about in my lifetime, judging from black-and-white movies and Hopper paintings: since the pervasion of carpeting, all you hear when people walk by are their own noises—the flap of their raincoats, the jingle of their change, the squeak of their shoes, the efficient little sniffs they make to signal to us and to themselves that they are busy and walking somewhere for a very good reason, as well as the almost sonic whoosh of receptionists' staggering and misguided perfumes, and the covert chokings and showings of tongues and placing of braceleted hands to windpipes that more tastefully scented secretaries exchange in their wake. One or two individuals in every office (Dave in mine), who have special pounding styles of walking, may still manage to get their footfalls heard; but in general now we all glide at work: a major improvement, as anyone knows who has visited those areas of offices that are still for various reasons linoleum-squared—cafeterias, mail-rooms, computer rooms. Linoleum was bearable back when incandescent light was there to counteract it with a softening glow, but the combination of fluorescence and linoleum, which must have been widespread for several years as the two trends overlapped, is not good.

As I had worked, then, my foot had, without any sanction from my conscious will, slipped from the untied shoe and sought out the texture of the carpeting; although now, as I reconstruct the moment, I realize that a more specialized desire was at work as well: when you slide a socked foot over a carpeted surface, the fibers of sock and carpet mesh and lock, so that though you think you are enjoying the texture of the carpeting, you are really enjoying the slippage of the inner surface of the sock against the underside of your foot, something you normally get to experience only in the morning when you first pull the sock on.[1]

At a few minutes before twelve, I stopped working, threw out my earplugs and, more carefully, the remainder of my morning coffee—placing it upright within the converging spinnakers of the trash can liner on the base of the receptacle itself. I stapled a copy of a memo someone had cc:'d me on to a copy of an earlier memo I had written on the same subject, and

[1] When I pull a sock on, I no longer *pre-bunch,* that is, I don't gather the sock up into telescoped folds over my thumbs and then position the resultant donut over my toes, even though I believed for some years that this was a clever trick, taught by admirable, fresh-faced kindergarten teachers, and that I revealed my laziness and my inability to plan ahead by instead holding the sock by the ankle rim and jamming my foot to its destination, working the ankle a few times to properly seat the heel. Why? The more elegant pre-bunching can leave in place any pieces of grit that have embedded themselves in your sole from the imperfectly swept floor you walked on to get from the shower to your room; while the cruder, more direct method, though it risks tearing an older sock, does detach this grit during the foot's downward passage, so that you seldom later feel irritating particles rolling around under your arch as you depart for the subway.

wrote at the top to my manager, in my best casual scrawl, "Abe—should I keep hammering on these people or drop it?" I put the stapled papers in one of my Eldon trays, not sure whether I would forward them to Abelardo or not. Then I slipped my shoe back on by flipping it on its side, hooking it with my foot, and shaking it into place. I accomplished all this by foot-feel; and when I crouched forward, over the papers on my desk, to reach the untied shoelace, I experienced a faint surge of pride in being able to tie a shoe without looking at it. At that moment, Dave, Sue, and Steve, on their way to lunch, waved as they passed by my office. Right in the middle of tying a shoe as I was, I couldn't wave nonchalantly back, so I called out a startled, overhearty "Have a good one, guys!" They disappeared; I pulled the left shoelace tight, and *bingo,* it broke.

The curve of incredulousness and resignation I rode out at that moment was a kind caused in life by a certain class of events, disruptions of physical routines, such as:

(a) reaching a top step but thinking there is another step there, and stamping down on the landing;
(b) pulling on the red thread that is supposed to butterfly a Band-Aid and having it wrest free from the wrapper without tearing it;
(c) drawing a piece of Scotch tape from the roll that resides half sunk in its black, weighted Duesenberg of a dispenser, hearing the slightly descending whisper of adhesive-coated plastic detaching itself from the back of the tape to come (descending in pitch because the strip, while amplifying the sound, is also getting longer as you pull on it[1]), and then, just as you are intending to break the piece off over the metal serration, reaching the innermost end of the roll, so that the segment you have been pulling wafts unexpectedly free. Especially now, with the rise of Post-it notes, which have made the massive black tape-dispensers seem even more grandiose and Biedermeier and tragically defunct, you almost believe that you will never come to the

[1] When I was little I thought it was called Scotch tape because the word "scotch" imitated the descending screech of early cellophane tapes. As incandescence gave way before fluorescence in office lighting, Scotch tape, once yellowish-transparent, became bluish-transparent, as well as superbly quiet.

end of a roll of tape; and when you do, there is a feeling, nearly, though very briefly, of shock and grief;

(d) attempting to staple a thick memo, and looking forward, as you begin to lean on the brontosaural head of the stapler arm,[1] to the three phases of the act—

> *first*, before the stapler arm makes contact with the paper, the resistance of the spring that keeps the arm held up; then, *second*, the moment when the small independent unit in the stapler arm noses into the paper and begins to force the two points of the staple into and through it; and, *third*, the felt crunch, like the chewing of an ice cube, as the twin tines of the staple emerge from the underside of the paper and are bent by the two troughs of the template in the stapler's base, curving inward in a crab's embrace of your memo, and finally disengaging from the machine completely—

but finding, as you lean on the stapler with your elbow locked and your breath held and it slumps toothlessly to the paper, that it has run out of staples. How could something this consistent, this incremental, betray you? (But then you are consoled: you get to reload it, laying bare the stapler arm and dropping a long zithering row of staples into place; and later, on the phone, you get to toy with the piece of the staples you couldn't fit into the stapler, breaking it into smaller segments, making them dangle on a hinge of glue.)

In the aftermath of the broken-shoelace disappointment, irrationally, I pictured Dave, Sue, and Steve as I had just seen them and thought, "Cheerful assholes!" because I had proba-

[1] Staplers have followed, lagging by about ten years, the broad stylistic changes we have witnessed in train locomotives and phonograph tonearms, both of which they resemble. The oldest staplers are cast-ironic and upright, like coal-fired locomotives and Edison wax-cylinder players. Then, in mid-century, as locomotive manufacturers discovered the word "streamlined," and as tonearm designers housed the stylus in aerodynamic ribbed plastic hoods that looked like trains curving around a mountain, the people at Swingline and Bates tagged along, instinctively sensing that staplers were like locomotives in that the two prongs of the staple make contact with a pair of metal hollows, which, like the paired rails under the wheels of the train, forces them to follow a preset path, and that they were like phonograph tonearms in that both machines, roughly the same size, make sharp points of contact with their respective media of informational storage. (In the case of the tonearm, the stylus retrieves the information, while in the case of the stapler, the staple binds it together as a unit—the order, the shipping paper, the invoice: *boom*, stapled, a unit; the letter of complaint, the copies of canceled checks and receipts, the letter of apologetic response: *boom*, sta-

bly broken the shoelace by transferring the social energy that I had had to muster in order to deliver a chummy "Have a good one!" to them from my awkward shoe-tier's crouch into the force I had used in pulling on the shoelace. Of course, it would have worn out sooner or later anyway. It was the original shoelace, and the shoes were the very ones my father had bought me two years earlier, just after I had started this job, my first out of college—so the breakage was a sentimental milestone of sorts. I rolled back in my chair to study the damage, imagining the smiles on my three co-workers' faces suddenly vanishing if I had really called them cheerful assholes, and regretting this burst of ill feeling toward them.

As soon as my gaze fell to my shoes, however, I was reminded of something that should have struck me the instant the shoelace had first snapped. The day before, as I had been getting ready for work, my *other* shoelace, the right one, had snapped, too, as I was yanking it tight to tie it, under very similar circumstances. I repaired it with a knot, just as I was planning to do now with the left. I was surprised—more than surprised—to think that after almost two years my right and left shoelaces could fail less than two days apart. Apparently my shoe-tying routine was so unvarying and robotic that over those hundreds of mornings I had inflicted identical levels of wear on both laces. The near simultaneity was very exciting—it made the variables of private life seem suddenly graspable and law-abiding.

---

pled, a unit; a sequence of memos and telexes holding the history of some interdepartmental controversy: *boom*, stapled, one controversy. In old stapled problems, you can see the TB vaccine marks in the upper left corner where staples have been removed and replaced, removed and replaced, as the problem—even the staple holes of the problem—was copied and sent on to other departments for further action, copying, and stapling.) And then the great era of squareness set in: BART was the ideal for trains, while AR and Bang & Olufsen turntables became angular—no more cream-colored bulbs of plastic! The people at Bates and Swingline again were drawn along, ridding their devices of all softening curvatures and offering black rather than the interestingly textured tan. And now, of course, the high-speed trains of France and Japan have reverted to aerodynamic profiles reminiscent of *Popular Science* cities-of-the-future covers of the fifties; and soon the stapler will incorporate a toned-down pompadour swoop as well. Sadly, the tonearm's stylistic progress has slowed, because all the buyers who would appreciate an up-to-date Soviet Realism in the design are buying CD players: its inspirational era is over.

I moistened the splayed threads of the snapped-off piece and twirled them gently into a damp, unwholesome minaret. Breathing steadily and softly through my nose, I was able to guide the saliva-sharpened leader thread through the eyelet without too much trouble. And then I grew uncertain. In order for the shoelaces to have worn to the breaking point on almost the same day, they would have had to be tied almost exactly the same number of times. But when Dave, Sue, and Steve passed my office door, I had been in the middle of tying one shoe—*one shoe only.* And in the course of a normal day it wasn't at all unusual for one shoe to come untied independent of the other. In the morning, of course, you always tied both shoes, but random midday comings-undone would have to have constituted a significant proportion of the total wear on both of these broken laces, I felt—possibly thirty percent. And how could I be positive that this thirty percent was equally distributed—that right and left shoes had come randomly undone over the last two years with the same frequency?

I tried to call up some sample memories of shoe-tying to determine whether one shoe tended to come untied more often than another. What I found was that I did not retain a single specific engram of tying a shoe, or a pair of shoes, that dated from any later than when I was four or five years old, the age at which I had first learned the skill. Over twenty years of empirical data were lost forever, a complete blank. But I suppose this is often true of moments of life that are remembered as major advances: the discovery is the crucial thing, not its repeated later applications. As it happened, the first *three* major advances in my life—and I will list all the advances here—

1. shoe-tying
2. pulling up on Xs
3. steadying hand against sneaker when tying
4. brushing tongue as well as teeth
5. putting on deodorant after I was fully dressed
6. discovering that sweeping was fun
7. ordering a rubber stamp with my address on it to make bill-paying more efficient
8. deciding that brain cells ought to die

—have to do with shoe-tying, but I don't think that this fact is very unusual. Shoes are the first adult machines we are given to master. Being taught to tie them was not like watching some adult fill the dishwasher and then being asked in a kind voice if you would like to clamp the dishwasher door shut and advance the selector knob (with its uncomfortable grinding sound) to Wash. That was artificial, whereas you knew that adults wanted you to learn how to tie your shoes; it was no fun for them to kneel. I made several attempts to learn the skill, but it was not until my mother placed a lamp on the floor so that I could clearly see the dark laces of a pair of new dress shoes that I really mastered it; she explained again how to form the introductory platform knot, which began high in the air as a frail, heart-shaped loop, and shrunk as you pulled the plastic lace-tips down to a short twisted kernel three-eighths of an inch long, and she showed me how to progress from that base to the main cotyledonary string figure, which was, as it turned out, not a true knot but an illusion, a trick that you performed on the lace-string by bending segments of it back on themselves and tightening other temporary bends around them: it looked like a knot and functioned like a knot, but the whole thing was really an amazing interdependent pyramid scheme, which much later I connected with a couplet of Pope's:

> Man, like the gen'rous vine, supported lives;
> The strength he gains is from th'embrace he gives.

Only a few weeks after I learned the basic skill, my father helped me to my second major advance, when he demonstrated thoroughness by showing me how to tighten the rungs of the shoelaces one by one, beginning down at the toe and working up, hooking an index finger under each X, so that by the time you reached the top you were rewarded with surprising lengths of lace to use in tying the knot, and at the same time your foot felt tightly papoosed and alert.

The third advance I made by myself in the middle of a playground, when I halted, out of breath, to tie a sneaker,[1] my

[1] Sneaker knots were quite different from dress knots—when you pulled the two loops tight at the end, the logic of the knot you had just created became untraceable; while in the case of dress-lace knots, you could, even

mouth on my interesting-smelling knee, a close-up view of anthills and the tread marks of other sneakers before me (the best kind, Keds, I think, or Red Ball Flyers, had a perimeter of asymmetrical triangles, and a few concavities in the center which printed perfect domes of dust), and found as I retied the shoe that I was doing it automatically, without having to concentrate on it as I had done at first, and, more important, that somewhere over the past year since I had first learned the basic moves, I had evidently evolved two little substeps of my own *that nobody had showed me.* In one I held down a temporarily taut stretch of shoelace with the side of my thumb; in the other I stabilized my hand with a middle finger propped against the side of the sneaker during some final manipulations. The advance here was my recognition that I had independently developed refinements of technique in an area where nobody had indicated there were refinements to be found: I had personalized an already adult procedure.

---

after tightening, follow the path of the knot around with your mind, as if riding a roller coaster. You could imagine a sneaker-shoelace knot and a dress-shoelace knot standing side by side saying the Pledge of Allegiance: the dress-shoelace knot would pronounce each word as a grammatical unit, understanding it as more than a sound; the sneaker-shoelace knot would run the words together. The great advantage of sneakers, though, one of the many advantages, was that when you had tied them tightly, without wearing socks, and worn them all day, and gotten them wet, and you took them off before bed, your feet would display the impression of the chrome eyelets in red rows down the sides of your foot, like the portholes in a Jules Verne submarine.

Chapter Three

PROGRESS LIKE THAT did not come again until I was over twenty. The fourth of the eight advances I have listed (to bring us quickly up to date, before we return to the broken shoelaces) came when I learned in college that L. brushed her tongue as well as her teeth. I had always imagined that tooth-brushing was an activity confined strictly to the teeth, possibly the gums—but I had sometimes felt fleeting doubts that cleaning merely those parts of your mouth really attacked the source of bad breath, which I held to be the tongue. I developed the habit of pretending to cough, cupping my hand over my lips to sniff my breath; when the results disturbed me, I ate celery. But soon after I began going out with L., she, shrugging as if it were a matter of common knowledge, told me that she brushed her tongue every day, with her toothbrush. I shivered with revulsion at first, but was very impressed. It wasn't until three years had passed that I too began brushing my own tongue regularly. By the time my shoelaces broke, I was regularly brushing not only my tongue but the roof of my mouth—and I am not exaggerating when I say that it is a major change in my life.

The fifth major advance was my discovery of a way to apply deodorant in the morning while fully dressed, an incident I will describe in more detail later on, since it occurred on the very morning I became an adult. (In my case, adulthood itself was not an advance, although it was a useful waymark.)

My second apartment after college was the scene of the sixth advance. The bedroom had a wooden floor. Someone at work (Sue) told me that she was depressed, but that she would go home and clean her apartment, because that always cheered her up. I thought, how strange, how mannerist, how interestingly contrary to my own instincts and practices—deliberately cleaning your apartment to alter your mood! A few weeks later, I came home on a Sunday afternoon after staying over at L.'s apartment. I was extremely cheerful, and after a few minutes of reading, I stood up with the decision that I would clean my room. (I lived in a house with four other people, and thus had only one room that was truly mine.) I picked up articles of clothing and threw some papers out; then I asked myself what people like L., or the depressed woman at work, did next. They swept. In the kitchen closet I found a practically new broom (not one of the contemporary designs, with synthetic bristles uniformly cut at an angle, but one just like the kind I had grown up with, with blond smocked twigs bound to a blue handle by perfectly wrapped silver wire) that one of my housemates had bought. I got to work, reminded of a whole chain of subsidiary childhood discoveries, such as putting to use one of my father's shirt cardboards as a dustpan, and bracing the broom with an armpit in order to sweep the dust one-handed onto the shirt cardboard; and I found that the act of sweeping around the legs of the chair and the casters of the stereo cabinet and the corners of the bookcase, outlining them with my curving broom-strokes, as if I were putting each chair leg and caster and doorjamb in quotation marks, made me see these familiar features of my room with freshened receptivity. The phone rang just as I had swept up a final pile of dust, coins, and old earplugs—the moment when the room was at its very cleanest, because the pile that I had just assembled was still there as evidence. It was L. I told her that I was sweeping my room, and that even though I had already been feeling very cheerful, this sweeping was making me wildly cheerful! She said that she had just swept her apartment, too. She said that for her the best moment was sweeping the dust into the dustpan, and getting those ruler-edged gray lines of superfine residue, one after another, diminishing in thickness toward invisibility, but never completely disappearing, as you backed the dustpan up. The fact that we had independently decided to sweep our apartments on that Sunday afternoon after spending the weekend together, I took as a strong piece of evidence that we were right for each other. And from then on when I read things Samuel Johnson said about the deadliness of leisure and the uplifting effects of industry, I always nodded and thought of brooms.

Advance number seven, occurring not long after the Sunday sweep, was occasioned by my ordering a rubber stamp with my name and address on it from an office-supply store, so that I wouldn't have to write out my return address repeatedly when I paid bills. I had dropped some things off at the cleaner's that day, and the day before I had taken some chairs that L. had inherited from an aunt to be recaned by blind people in a distant suburb; I also had written my grandparents, and I had ordered a transcript of a MacNeil-Lehrer show in which an interviewee had said things that represented with particular clarity a way of thinking I disagreed with, and I had sent off to Penguin, just as they suggested in the back of all their paperbacks, for a "complete list of books available"; two days earlier I had dropped off my shoes to be reheeled—it's amazing that heels wear down before the laces snap—and paid several bills (which had made me think of the need for an address stamp). As I walked out of the office-supply store, I became aware of the power of all these individual, simultaneously pending transactions: all over the city, and at selected sites in other states, events were being set in motion on my behalf, services were being performed, simply because I had requested them and in some cases paid or agreed to pay later for them. (The letter to my grandparents didn't exactly fit, but contributed to the feeling even so.) Molten rubber was soon to be poured into backward metal letters that spelled my name and address; blind people were making clarinetists' finger motions over the holes of a half-caned chair, gauging distances and degrees of tautness; somewhere in the Midwest in rooms full of Tandem computers and Codex statistical multiplexers the magnetic record of certain debts in my name was being overwritten with a new magnetic record that corresponded to a figure diminished to the penny by the amount that I had written out in hasty felt-tip pen on my checks (I made the traditional long wavy mark after "and $^{00}/_{100}$" on the dollar line, just as my parents had, and their parents had before them); the dry cleaner's would close soon, and in a sack somewhere in the darkened store, tied in a bundle to keep it separate from all other bundles, behind the faded posters in the window saying "For That Newly Tailored Look," my dirty clothing would rest for the night; I trusted them to take temporary possession of it, and they trusted me to return to their store and pay them for making it look like new. All of this and more I could get the world to do for me, and at the same time all of it was going on, I could walk down the street, unburdened with the niceties of the individual tasks, living my life! I felt like an efficient short-order cook, having eight or nine different egg orders working at once, dropping the toast, rolling the sausages, setting up the plates, flicking the switch that illuminated a waitress's number. It was the rubber stamp specifically that pushed the advance over the top, because, in bearing my name, the stamp summed up all of this action at a distance, and was itself a secondary, life-ordering act, which had taken time now, but which would save time later, *every bill I paid.*

The eighth advance, the last one that I can think of antedating the day of the broken laces, was a set of four reasons why it was a good thing for brain cells to die. One way or another, I had worried about the death of brain cells since I was about ten, convinced year after year that I was getting more stupid; and when I began to drink in a small way, and the news broke (while I was in college) that an ounce of distilled spirits kills one thousand neurons (I think that was the ratio), the concern intensified. One weekend I confessed to my mother on the phone that I had been worrying that over the past six months especially, my brain wattage had dimmed perceptibly. She had always been interested in materialist analogies for cognition, and she offered reassurance, as I knew she would. "It's true," she said, "that your individual brain cells are dying, but the ones that stay grow more and more connections, and those connections keep branching out over the years, and that's the progress you have to keep in mind. It's the number of links that are important, not the raw number of cells." This observation was exceedingly helpful. In the week or two following her news that connections continued to proliferate in the midst of neural carnage, I formed several related theories:

(a) We begin, perhaps, with a brain that is much too crowded with pure processing capacity, and therefore the death of the brain cells is part of a *planned and necessary* winnowing that precedes the move upward to higher levels of intelligence: the weak ones fizzle out, and the gaps they leave as they are reabsorbed stimulate the growth buds of dendrites, which now have more capacious playgrounds, and complex correlational structures come about as a result. (Or perhaps the dendrites' own heightened need for space to grow forces a mating struggle: they lock antlers with feebler outriggers in the search for the informationally rich connections, shortcutting through intermediate territories and causing them to wither and shut down like neighborhoods near a new thruway.) With fewer total cells, but more connections between each cell, the quality of your knowledge undergoes a transformation: you begin to have a feel for situations, people fall into types, your past memories link together, and your life begins to seem, as it hadn't when you were younger, an inevitable thing composed of a million small failures and successes dependently intergrown, as opposed to a bright beadlike row of unaffiliated moments. Mathematicians need all of those spare neurons, and their careers falter when the neurons do, but the rest of us should be thankful for their disappearance, for it makes room for experience. Depending on where on the range you began, you are shifted as your brain ages toward the richer, more mingled pole: mathematicians become philosophers, philosophers become historians, historians become biographers, biographers become college provosts, college provosts become political consultants, and political consultants run for office.

(b) Used with care, substances that harm neural tissue, such as alcohol, can aid intelligence: you corrode the chromium, giggly, crossword puzzle–solving parts of your mind with pain and poison, forcing the neurons to take responsibility for themselves and those around them, toughening themselves against the accelerated wear of these artificial solvents. After a night of poison, your brain wakes up in the morning saying, "No, I don't give a shit who introduced the sweet potato into North America." The damage that you have inflicted heals over, and the scarred places left behind have unusual surface areas, roughnesses enough to become the nodes around which wisdom weaves its fibrils.

(c) The neurons that do expire are the ones that made imitation possible. When you are capable of skillful imitation, the sweep of choices before you is too large; but when your brain loses its spare capacity, and along with it some agility, some joy in winging it, and the ambition to do things that don't suit it, then you finally have to settle down to do well the few things that your brain really can do well—the rest no longer seems pressing and distracting, because it is now permanently out of reach. The feeling that you are stupider than you were is what finally interests you in the really complex subjects of life: in change, in experience, in the ways other people have adjusted to disappointment and narrowed ability. You realize that you are no prodigy, your shoulders relax, and you begin to look around you, seeing local color unrivaled by blue glows of algebra and abstraction.

(d) Individual ideas are injured along with the links over which they travel. As they are dismembered and remembered, damaged, forgotten, and later refurbished, they become subtler, more hierarchical, tiered with half-obliterated particulars. When they molder or sustain damage, they regenerate more as a part of the self, and less as a part of an external system.

These were the eight main advances I had available to bring to bear on my life on the day I sat repairing the second shoelace to wear out in two days.

Chapter Four

After I had finished the repair knot, a lump with two frizzed ends just below the top pair of eyelets, I pulled on the tongue of the shoe—another of the little preludes to tying that my father had shown me—and gingerly began the regulation knot. I took special care to scale down the bunny's ear that I had to form from the now shorter lace-end, so that there would be enough leeway to pull it tight without mishap.[1] I watched with interest the fluent, thoughtless fumblings of my hands: they were the hands of a mature person, with vein-work and a fair amount of hair on their backs, but they had learned these moves so well and so long ago that elements of a much earlier gilled and tailed self seemed to persist in them. I noticed my shoes, too, for the first time in quite a while. They were no longer new-looking: I thought of them still as new, because I had more or less begun my job with them, but now I saw that they had two deep wrinkle lines above the toe, intersectingly angled, like the line of the heart and the line of the head in palmistry. These creases had always appeared on

[1] Not liking when you end up with only one of the two bunny's ears that make up a normal bow; for if for some reason the lace-end forming that one ear works free, you have no backup and you end up with a granny or square knot that you have to tease untied with your fingernails, blood rushing to your head.

my shoes in exactly the same form, a puzzling fact that I had thought about often when I was little—I had tried to accelerate the forming of the paired wrinkles by bending a new shoe manually, and I had wondered why, if the shoe had just happened to begin to bend in a certain atypical place, because of a fluke weakness in the leather there, it never established the wrinkle line where it had first bent, but eventually assumed the classic sideways V pattern.

I stood, rolled my chair back into place, and took a step toward my office door, where my jacket hung all day, unused except when the air-conditioning became violent or I had a presentation to give; but as soon as I felt myself take that step, I experienced a sharpening of dissatisfaction with the whole notion that my daily acts of shoe-tying could have alone worn out my shoelaces. What about the variety of tiny stretchings and pullings that the shoe itself exerted on its laces as I walked around? Walking was what had worn down my heels; walking was what had put the creases in my shoe-toes—was I supposed to discount the significance of walking in the chafing of my laces? I remembered shots in movies of a rope that held up a bridge cutting itself against a sharp rock as the bridge swayed. Even if the shoelace's fabric moved only millimetrically against its eyelet with each step, that sawing back and forth might eventually cut through the outer fibers, though the lace would not actually pop until a relatively large force, such as the first tug I gave it when tying, was applied.

All right! Much better! This walking-flexion model (as I styled it to myself, in opposition to the earlier pulling-and-fraying model) accounted for the coincidence of yesterday's and today's breakages very well, I thought. I almost never hopped, or lounged in a storefront with one foot crossing one ankle, or otherwise flexed one foot to the exclusion of the other—patterns of use that would have worn one shoelace disproportionately. I *had* slipped on a curb's icy wheelchair ramp the year before, and had used a crutch the next day, favoring my left leg for a week after that, but five days of limping was probably insignificant, and anyway, I wasn't at all sure that I had worn these, my new and best, shoes that week, since I wouldn't have wanted to get mountain-range salt-stains on the toes.

Still, I reflected, if it were true that the laces frayed from walking flexion, why did they invariably fray only in contact with the top pair of eyelets on each shoe? I paused in my doorway, looking out at the office, with my hand resting on the concave metal doorknob,[1] resisting this further un-

[1] Too modern-looking, really, to be called a door*knob*. Why can't office buildings use doorknobs that are truly knob-like in shape? What is this static modernism that architects of the second tier have imposed on us: steel half-U handles or lathed objects shaped like superdomes, instead of brass, porcelain, or glass knobs? The upstairs doorknobs in the house I grew up in were made of faceted glass. As you extended your fingers to open a door, a cloud of flesh-color would diffuse into the glass from the opposite direction. The knobs were loosely seated in their latch mechanism, and heavy, and the combination of solidity and laxness made for a multiply staged experience as you turned the knob: a smoothness that held intermediary tumbleral fallings-into-position. Few American products recently have been able to capture that same knuckly, orthopedic quality (the quality of bendable straws) in their switches and latches; the Japanese do it very well, though: they can get a turn-signal switch in a car or a volume knob on a stereo to feel resistant and substantial and *worn into place*—think of the very fine Toyota turn-signal switches, to the left of the steering wheel, which move in their sockets like chicken drumsticks: they feel as if they were designed with living elbow cartilage as their inspiration. But the 1905 doorknobs in our house had that quality. My father must have had special affection for them, because he draped his ties over them. Often you had to open a door carefully, holding the knob at its very edge, to avoid injuring the several ties that hung there. The whole upstairs had the air of a nawab's private chambers; as you closed a bedroom, bathroom, or closet door, a heavy plume of richly variegated silks would swing out and sway back silently; once in a while a tie would ripple to the floor, having been gradually cranked into disequilibrium by many turnings of the doorknob. If I asked to borrow a tie, when I was tall enough to wear them, my father was always delighted: he would tour the doorknobs, pulling promising ties out carefully and displaying them against his forearm, as sommeliers hold their arm-cloths. "Here's a beautiful tie. . . . Now this is a very subtle tie. . . . What about this tie?" He taught me the principal classifications: rep tie, neat tie, paisley tie. And the tie I wore for the job interview at the company on the mezzanine was one he had pulled from a doorknob: it was made of a silk that verged on crepe, and its pattern was composed of very small oval shapes, each containing a fascinating blob motif that seemed inspired by the hungry, pulsating amoebas that absorbed excess stomach acid in Rolaids' great dripping-faucet commercial, and when you looked closely you noticed that the perimeter of each oval was made of surprisingly garishly colored rectangles, like suburban tract houses; a border so small in scale, however, that those instances of brightness only contributed a secret depth and luminosity to the overall somber, old-masters coloration of the design. My father was able to find ties as outstanding as that even though he was himself slightly color-blind at the green end of the spectrum; on days when he was pitching a big client, he would appear in the kitchen in the morning with three ties he had selected and ask us—my mother, my

welcome puzzlement. I had never heard of a shoelace parting over some middle eyelet. Possibly the stress of walking fell most forcefully on the lace bent around the top eyelets, just as the stress of pulling the laces tight to tie them did. It was conceivable, though scary to imagine, that the pull-fray model and the walk-flex model mingled their coefficients so subtly that human agency would never accurately apportion cause.

I walked to Tina's cube, on the outside wall of which was the sign-out board, and moved the green magnetized puck next to my name from IN to OUT, bringing it in line with Dave's, Sue's, and Steve's pucks. I wrote "Lunch" in the space provided for explanation, using a green Magic Marker.

"Have you signed the poster for Ray?" said Tina, rolling out in her chair. Tina had lots of hair, moussed out impressively around a small smart face; she was probably at her most alert just then, because she was watching the phones for Deanne and Julie, the other secretaries in my department, until they

---

sister, and me—to choose the one that went best with his shirt: this constituted a sort of dry run for his imminent meeting, where he would also present three choices, mock-ups of eighteen-page sales promotion pieces or themes for trade-show slide presentations. When I had dinner with him and other relatives in the first year of my job, I wore the best tie I had bought to date; and as my uncle conferred with the hostess about the table, my father turned toward me, caught sight of my tie, and said, "Hey, hey—*nice*," fingering the silk. "Is this one of mine or one you bought?"

"I picked this one up a while ago, I guess," I said, pretending to think back with effort, when in fact I remembered every detail of the transaction; remembered carrying the very light, very expensive bag home not more than five weeks before.

"A 'neat' tie—a 'neat' tie." He lowered his glasses and bent to examine the pattern more closely—rows of paired lozenges intersecting like Venn diagrams, mostly red. "Very fine."

I said, "This is one I haven't seen before, have I?" fingering his tie in turn. "Really nice."

"This?" he said. He flipped it over, as if he too had to remind himself of the circumstances in which he had bought it. "I picked this up at Whillock Brothers."

As we were all seated at the table, I looked around at my male relatives' ties: at my grandfather's tie and my uncle's tie and my aunt's father's tie—and it was clear to me that my father and I were without question wearing the two best-looking ties at the table that night. A sudden balloon payment of pride and gratitude expanded within me. Later still, when I went home to visit, I swapped a tie with him, and when I visited the following Thanksgiving, I spotted what had been my tie hanging over a doorknob in the midst of all the ties he had bought himself, and it fit right in, it fit right in!

returned from lunch after one. In the more private area of her cube, in the shadow of the shelf under the unused fluorescent light, she had pinned up shots of a stripe-shirted husband, some nephews and nieces, Barbra Streisand, and a multiply xeroxed sentiment in Gothic type that read, "If You Can't Get Out of It, Get Into It!" I would love sometime to trace the progress of these support-staff sayings through the offices of the city; Deanne had another one pushpinned to a wall of her cube, its capitals in crumbling ruins under the distortion of so many copies of copies; it said, "YOU MEAN YOU WANT ME TO RUSH THE RUSH JOB I'M RUSHING TO RUSH?"

"What's happened to old Ray?" I said; Ray being the man responsible for emptying the trash in each office and cubicle and restocking the bathroom supplies, but not for vacuuming, which was done by an outside company. He was about forty-five, proud of his kids, wore plaid shirts—he was always associated for me with the feeling of working late, because I could hear the gradual approach of distant papery crashes and the slinkier sounds of sheet plastic as Ray worked his way down the row toward my office, emptying each wastebasket liner into a gray triangular plastic push-dumpster, and thereby defining that day as truly over for that office, even though you might still be working in it, because anything you now threw out was *tomorrow's trash.* Before he draped a new plastic liner in a wastebasket, he left a second, folded one cached in the bottom for the next day, saving himself a few motions on every stop; and he tied a very fast knot in the plastic so that it wouldn't be pulled in, effectively becoming trash itself, as soon as you discarded something big like a newspaper.

"He hurt his back last weekend while trying to move a swimming pool," said Tina.

I winced in office sympathy. "An above-ground pool, I hope."

"A toddler's pool for his grandniece. He may be out for a while."

"That explains why for the last few days, whenever I throw out my coffee cup, I've had to lower it through this puffy cushion of plastic. The person who's been taking Ray's place doesn't know how to get rid of the trapped air. I've been kind of enjoying the effect, though—a pillow effect."

"I'll bet you enjoy the pillow effect," she said, flirting mechanically. She led me to a poster laid out on the desk of a research assistant who had called in sick.

"I sign where?"

"Anywhere. Here's a pen."

I had already half pulled out my shirt-pocket pen, but not wanting to refuse her offer, I hesitated; at the same time, she saw that I already had a pen, and with an "Oh" began to retract hers from the proffering position; meanwhile I had decided to accept hers and had let go of the one in my pocket, not registering until it was too late that she had withdrawn the offer; she, seeing that I was now beginning to reach for her pen, canceled her retraction, but meanwhile I, processing her earlier corrective movement, had gone back to reaching for my own pen—so we went through a little foilwork that was like the mutual bobbings you exchange with an oncoming pedestrian, as both of you lurch to indicate whether you are going to pass to the right or to the left. Finally I took her pen and studied the poster; it depicted, in felt-tip colors, a vase holding five large, loopy outlined flowers. On the vase was the legend, in A+ cursive handwriting, "Ray, missing you, hoping you come back to work soon! From your Co-Workers." And on the petals of the felt-tip flowers were the neat, nearly identical signatures of many secretaries from the mezzanine, all of them signed at different angles. Intermixed with these were the more varied signatures of a few of the managers and research assistants. I made an exclamation about its beauty: it *was* beautiful.

"Julie did the vase, I did the flowers," said Tina.

I found an unobtrusive petal of the fourth flower: not too prominent, because I had a feeling that I might have been a little on the cool side to Ray recently—you go through inevitable cycles of office friendliness—and I wanted him to see signatures of people whose sentiments he would be absolutely sure of first. I almost signed, and then luckily I noticed that my boss Abelardo's tall and horizontally compressed conquistador signature, with lots of overloops and proud flourishes, was located one petal over on the very same flower I had chosen. To sign my name so near his would have been vaguely wrong: it might be construed as the assertion of a special alliance (my signature being closer than Dave's or Sue's or Steve's, who also worked for Abelardo), or it might seem to imply that I was seeking out my boss's name because I wanted to be near another exempt person's name, avoiding the secretarial signatures. I had signed enough office farewell and birthday and get-well cards by that time to have developed an unhealthy sensitivity to the nuances of signature placement. I moved over to an antipodal flower's petal, near Deanne's name, and signed at what I hoped was an original angle. "Ray will sob with joy when he sees this poster, Tina," I said.

"Aren't you nice," said Tina. "Lunchtime?"

"Off to buy shoelaces. One broke yesterday and one broke just now. Doesn't that seem strangely coincidental to you? I don't know how to explain it."

Tina frowned for a moment and then pointed at me. "You know, it's interesting you say that, because we have two smoke detectors in our house, all right? We've had them since about a year ago. Last week, the battery of one of them wore down, and it started to go, 'Peep! . . . peep! . . . peep!' So Russ went out and bought a new battery. And then the very next day, in the morning, I was just on my way out the door, I've got my keys in my hand, and suddenly I hear, 'Peep! . . . peep! . . . peep!' from the other one. Two days in a row."

"That's very strange."

"It is. Especially because one of them goes off more often, because it's nearer the kitchen and it doesn't like it when I do any kind of broiling. Chicken roasting—peep, peep!—red alert! But the other one only went off once that I can remember."

"So you're saying it doesn't matter if they're used or not."

"Yeah, it doesn't matter. Wait a second." Her phone had begun ringing; she excused herself by raising her hand. Then, in a voice that was suddenly sweet, efficient, platinum-throated, slightly breathy, she said,

> "Good morning,[1] Donald Vanci's office? I'm sorry, Don's stepped away from his desk. May I take your number and have him get back to you?"

[1] Though by then it was by Tina's own desk clock 12:04 P.M. I was always touched when, out of a morning's worth of repetition, secretaries continued to answer with good mornings for an hour or so into the afternoon, just as

Smoothly disengaging her pen from my fingers, she located her While You Were Out pad and wrote down a name. Then, repeating product codes and amounts, she began to take a complex message. I wanted slightly to leave, but it would have been brusque to do so. What with Ray's poster and the roasting chicken, our interchange had passed just barely beyond office civility into the realm of human conversation, and thus had to be terminated conversationally: etiquette required me to wait until her phone duty was done in order to exchange one last sentence with her, unless the message she was taking was clearly going to go on for more than three minutes, in which case Tina, who knew the conventions well, would release me—cued first by some "Gee, I'm taking off now" movement from me (pulling up the pants, checking for my wallet, a joke salute)—with a mouthed "Bye!"

While I waited, I checked the revolving message carousel for messages, despite the fact that I had been in all morning and would have gotten any calls for me; then, reaching into Tina's cube, I picked up her heavy chrome date-stamper. It was a self-inking model: at rest, the internal dating element, looped with six belts of rubber, held its current numerology pressed upside down against the moist black roof of the armature. To use it, you set the square base of the machine down on the piece of paper you wished to date and pressed on the wooden knob (a true knob!)—then the internal element, guided by S curves cut out of the gantry-like superstructure, began its graceful rotational descent, uprighting itself just in time for landing like the lunar excursion module, touching the paper for an instant, depositing today's date, and then springing back up to its bat-repose. When I came in early in the morning, I sometimes watched (through the glass wall of my office) Tina advance the date of the date-stamper: after she had finished her plain donut, and had frisked the crumbs from her fingertips into the piece of plastic wrap that the donut had come in, and had folded the plastic wrap in around the crumbs until it formed a neat whitish pellet, and had thrown the pellet out,

---

people often date things with the previous year well into February; sometimes they caught their mistake and went into a "This is not my day" or "Where is my head?" escape routine; but in a way they were right, since the true tone of afternoons does not take over in offices until nearly two.

she would unlock her desk and remove her stapler, her While You Were Out pad (these tended to disappear if you didn't hide them), and the date-stamper from her meticulously arranged central drawer, placing any extra packets of sweetener that the deli had thrown in with her coffee into a special partition in the drawer that contained nothing but sweetener packets. And then she would advance the rubber belt of the date-stamper by a single digit, a performance that by now probably began the day for her, as her first office act—just as my turning ahead my Page-A-Day calendar, with its two hoops of metal over which you guided the holes of the postcard-sized page, to the next day (which I always did last thing the night before, because I found it deflating to confront yesterday's appointments and "to do's" first thing in the morning) had become the escapement on which my own life ratcheted forward.

Now I touched the date-stamper's belts of rubber numbers, which were updated by little metal thumb-wheels; the belts that corresponded to days were entirely black, but the belt that corresponded to the decade was still red-rubber-colored and new, except for the 8, which was sticky with ink. I opened my palm and pressed the date into it.

"Let me read those figures back to you," Tina was saying. The interesting thing about having to stand there and wait for her to finish before I left for lunch was that, even though we had been in the middle of a conversation whose interrupted momentum was what was holding me there, the longer I stood, the less likely it became that we would resume where we had left off, not because we had forgotten the thread, but because we had been discussing light, dismissable subjects, and neither of us wanted to be perceived as having paid too close attention to them: we wanted to preserve their status as chance observations that we had happened to make in the midst of a hundred other equally interesting items in our lives we might just as easily have mentioned to each other. And indeed, when Tina finally hung up, she said, changing instantly from her telephone voice, sensing that I wanted to get going, "How is it out there?" She leaned back to look at the square of blue sky and two taut, vibrating pulley-ropes from the window-washer's gondola visible through her boss's window.[1] "Ooh, it's gorgeous out," she said. "I've got so many things to do—Julie better be back on time. I've got to get a birthday present for my goddaughter, a card for Mother's Day . . ."

"Oh man, that's coming up."

"Yep, and I've got to get a flea collar for my dog, and what else? There was something else."

"A battery for your second smoke alarm."

"That's right! No, actually Russ bought extras. He's smart, you know?"

"Smart guy," I said, tapping my temple as she had. "Tell me one thing—where would I get shoelaces?"

"CVS, maybe? There's a shoe repair place over by Delicato's—no, that's closed. CVS would definitely have them, I think."

"All righty!" I put down the date-stamper in its correct position on her desktop. "Bye."

"Did you sign out?"

I said I had.

She wagged her finger at me. "I have to watch you every minute. Have a nice lunch!"[2]

I stepped away toward the men's room, and the lunch hour beyond.

[1] Really it wasn't blue sky at all, but green; the reflective layer of the glass shifted colors from true, and that change, combined with the hiss from the registers below each window, made the sky seem very distant, and the outside temperature hard to guess. I had noticed that it was not considered cool to make any remarks about the window-washers if they rose past while you were talking to a co-worker; everyone was supposed to be so used to them that they couldn't possibly elicit a joke or a comment.

[2] There are two ideal ways to wind up a light conversation with a co-worker; one is with a little near-joke, and the other is with the exchange of a piece of useful information. The first is more common, but the second is preferable. The chat with Tina was the longest conversation I had had yet that day (and, as it turned out, was to have that day, until L. called at nine in the evening—more than enough talk, though, oddly enough, to satisfy my midweek socializing instincts); and I was pleased that it had ended with her telling me that I could get shoelaces at CVS. It made us both feel we were moving ahead in our lives: at random, on errands of her own, she had learned something that other people apparently didn't know, and she was now passing the knowledge on to me.

Chapter Five

IT ISN'T RIGHT to say, "When I was little, I used to love *x*," if you still love *x* now. I admit that part of my pleasure in riding the escalator came from the links with childhood memory that the experience sustained. Other people remember liking boats, cars, trains, or planes when they were children—and I liked them too—but I was more interested in systems of local transport: airport luggage-handling systems (those overlapping new moons of hard rubber that allowed the moving track to turn a corner, neatly drawing its freight of compressed clothing with it; and the fringe of rubber strips that marked the transition between the bright inside world of baggage claim and the outside world of low-clearance vehicles and men in blue outfits); supermarket checkout conveyor belts, turned on and off like sewing machines by a foot pedal, with a seam like a zipper that kept reappearing; and supermarket roller coasters made of rows of vertical rollers arranged in a U curve over which the gray plastic numbered containers that held your bagged and paid-for groceries would slide out a flapped gateway to the outside; milk-bottling machines we saw on field trips that hurried the queueing bottles on curved tracks with rubber-edged side-rollers toward the machine that socked milk into them and clamped them with a paper cap; marble chutes; Olympic luge and bobsled tracks; the hanger-management systems at the dry cleaner's—sinuous circuits of rustling plastics (NOT A TOY! NOT A TOY! NOT A TOY!) and dimly visible clothing that looped from the customer counter way back to the pressing machines in the rear of the store, fanning sideways as they slalomed around old men at antique sewing machines who were making sense of the heap of random pairs of pants pinned with little notes; laundry lines that cranked clothes out over empty space and cranked them back in when the laundry was dry; the barbecue-chicken display at Woolworth's that rotated whole orange-golden chickens on pivoting skewers; and the rotating Timex watch displays, each watch box open like a clam; the cylindrical roller-cookers on which hot dogs slowly turned in the opposite direction to the rollers, blistering; gears that (as my father explained it) in their greased intersection modified forces and sent them on their way. The escalator shared qualities with all of these systems, with one difference: it was the only one I could get on and ride.

So my pleasure in riding the escalator that afternoon was partly a pleasure of indistinct memories and associations—and not only memories of my father's (and my own) world of mechanical enthusiasms, but memories also of my mother taking my sister and me to department stores and teaching us to approach the escalator with care. She warned me not to jam a wad of molar-textured pink gum into the gap between one curved riser and the grooved stair below it—I wanted to because I wanted to see the gum crushed with the dwarfing force of a large, steady machine, the way garbage trucks forced paper cartons to crumple into each other. She would lift my sister up as we stepped onto the escalator, pinning the noisy form of the shopping bag to herself with her elbow, and set her down on a higher stair. I couldn't comfortably hold the rubber handrail, and sensibly wasn't allowed to steady myself with the high step ahead of me. As we drew close to the next floor, I could see a green glow coming from under the crenellated slit where the escalator steps disappeared; and as soon as I stepped off, onto oddly immobile linoleum and then a tundra of carpeting, the soft sounds reached me from some department I knew nothing about, like the "Miss" department: clickings of hangers with metal hooks and plastic armatures, hangers that were not heavily loaded with men's anechoic wool suits but rather were shouldering light, knitted burdens in tight schoolgirl circles around a cardboard CLEARANCE sign, accompanied by the melodious signal of the "Miss" telephone, dinging in slow sets of fours, one ding every second.

Yet, though it is true that my thoughts about escalators now are composed of up to seventy or eighty percent of this kind of kid-memory, I have lately become increasingly uncomfortable about including it in descriptions of the things I love—and it was only a few weeks ago, several years after the escalator ride that is the vehicle of this memoir, that I reached a somewhat firmer position on the whole issue. I was driving south, in the middle lane of a wide highway, at about 7:45 in the morning, on a very blue, bright, snowless day in winter, on my way to the job that I had taken after leaving my job with the department on the mezzanine.[1] I had the sun-visor flap swung over to shield me from direct sunlight, which was hot on the left—in fact, I had extended the shade-range of the sun-visor (that beautiful aileron, notched in one corner to clear the rearview mirror) by slipping a manila folder over it—so the sky in front of me was filled with an excellent, pure blue, while no sun fell directly on me to make me squint. Cars and trucks around mine were all nicely spaced: close enough to create a sense of fellowship and shared purpose, but not close enough to make you think that you couldn't swerve exuberantly into another lane at any time if you wanted. I had the vertebrae of the steering wheel in my left hand and a Styrofoam cup of coffee with a special sipmaster top in my right.

I drew close behind a green truck going about five miles an hour slower than I was. It was technically a "garbage truck," but not the kind of city machine that comes to mind when you hear that phrase (the drooping rear section like the hairnet of a

[1] At the time I was riding the escalator to the mezzanine every day I didn't own a car, but later, when I did, I realized that escalatorial happiness is not too far removed from the standard pleasure that the highway commuter feels driving his warm, quiet box between pulsing intermittencies of white road paint at a steady speed.

food-service worker). It was, instead, the larger kind of truck that hauls the compressed garbage from some central processing site to a landfill: a big rectangular container drawn by a semi-detached cab. I know that the garbage was somehow compressed because I could see little pieces of it pressing fiercely out the slight gap under the rear panel—it was not refuse of a normal, fluffy, just-gathered density. Thick green canvas covers, very dirty, were drawn across the top of the container, secured with bungee lines that stretched in angles down its sides.

The angles of the bungee lines and the transition between those straight lines and the taut scalloped curves they pulled from the cloth covers were what pleased me first. Then I looked between the bungee lines at the surface of the metal container: organic shapes of rust had been painted over with more green, and the rust, still active, had continued to grow under its new coat, so that there was a combination of the freshness of recent paint and the hidden weatheredness of rust. The whole thing looked crisply beautiful as I changed lanes to pass it. Right when I suddenly had more blue sky in front of me than green truck, I remembered that when I was little I used to be very interested in the fact that anything, no matter how rough, rusted, dirty, or otherwise discredited it was, looked good if you set it down on a stretch of white cloth, or any kind of clean background. The thought came to me with just that prefix: "when I was little," along with the sight of a certain rusted railroad spike I had found and placed on an expanse of garage concrete that I had carefully swept smooth. (Garage dust fills in concrete's imperfections when you sweep with it, making a very smooth surface.) This clean-background trick, which I had come upon when I was eight or so, applied not only to things I owned, such as a group of fossil brachiopods I set against a white shirt cardboard, but also to things in museums: curators arranged geodes, early American eyeglasses, and boot scrapers against black or gray velvet backgrounds because anytime you set some detail of the world off that way, it was able to take on its true stature as an object of attention.

But it was the garbage truck I saw *at age thirty* on display against the blue sky that had reminded me of my old backdrop discovery. Though simple, the trick was something that struck me as interesting and useful *right now*. Thus, the "when I was little" nostalgia was misleading: it turned something that I was taking seriously as an adult into something soupier, less precise, more falsely exotic, than it really was. Why should we need lots of nostalgia to license any pleasure taken in the discoveries that we carry over from childhood, when it is now so clearly an adult pleasure? I decided that from now on I wouldn't get that faraway look when describing things that excited me now, regardless of whether they had first been childhood enthusiasms or not.

As if in reward for this resolution, later that same day I was looking in a cooler in a convenience store and saw a plastic-packaged sandwich labeled "Cream Cheese and Sliced Olive." The idea of a cross-section of olive-encircled pimiento set like a cockatoo's eye in the white stretch of cream cheese hit me very hard as an illustration of the same principle I had rediscovered that morning: on their own, olives are old, pickled, briny, rusty—but set them off against a background of cream cheese and you have jewelry.[1]

So I want now to do two things: to set the escalator to the mezzanine against a clean mental background as something fine and worth my adult time to think about, and to state that

[1] I was especially interested that the food service had inserted "sliced" in the title of their sandwich, perhaps on the model of "sliced egg sandwich." You don't have to say "tuna and *sliced* celery," or even "tuna and celery"; the reason we flag the existence of olives is that while the tuna is tan and crumbly and therefore aggregative, cream cheese is a unitary scrim, and the olives inset into it demand an equal billing. In truth, the question is less subtle than this: olives are a more powerful taste in a bed of cream cheese than celery is within the tangy disorder of tuna: celery is often used simply as an extender, texturing and adding a cheap chew-interest, while olives are more expensive ounce for ounce than cream cheese, and therefore demonstrate higher yearnings, nobler intentions. What can freshen and brighten that blandness? the food scientist asked himself, assigned the task of making a simple cream cheese sandwich appetizing. Mushrooms? Chives? Paprika? *And then*—he sliced one olive, worth maybe two cents wholesale, into six pieces, spaced them evenly in their white medium, and suddenly all the squinting, cackling, cocktail-wickedness of a narrow gourmet jar of Spanish olives in the door shelf of your refrigerator inhabited the cheapest, most innocent, most childlike sandwich you can make.

while I did draw some large percentage of joy from the continuities that the adult escalator ride established with childhood escalators, I will try not to glide on the reminiscential tone, as if only children had the capacity for wonderment at this great contrivance.

Chapter Six

WHILE STILL temporarily intoxicated by this sensation of candor, I have to say that no matter how hard I try to keep sentimental distortions from creeping in, they creep in anyway. In the case of the escalator, I can probably keep the warpage down, because escalators have been around, unchanging (except for that exciting season when glass-sided escalators appeared), for my whole life—nothing has been lost. But other things, like gas pumps, ice cube trays, transit buses, or milk containers, have undergone disorienting changes, and the only way that we can understand the proportion and range and effect of those changes, which constitute the often undocumented daily texture of our lives (a rough, gravelly texture, like the shoulder of a road, which normally passes too fast for microscopy), is to sample early images of the objects in whatever form they take in kid-memory—and once you invoke those kid-memories, you have to live with their constant tendency to screw up your fragmentary historiography with violas of lost emotion. I drink milk very rarely now; in fact, the half-pint carton I bought at Papa Gino's to go with the cookie was one of the very last times: it was a sort of test to see whether I still could drink it with the old pleasure. (You have to spot-check your likes and dislikes every so often in this way to see whether your reactions have altered, I think.) But I continue to admire the milk carton, and I believe that the change from milk delivered to the door in bottles to milk bought at the supermarket in cardboard containers with peaked roofs was a significant change for people roughly my age—younger and you would have allied yourself completely with the novelty as your starting point and felt no loss;[1] older and you would have already exhausted your faculties of regret on earlier minor transitions and shrugged at this change. Because I grew up as the tradition evolved, I have an awe, still, of the milk carton, which brought milk into supermarkets where all the rest of the food was, in boxes of wax-treated cardboard that said "Sealtest," a nice laboratorial word. I first saw the invention in the refrigerator at my best friend Fred's house (I don't know how old I was, possibly five or six): the radiant idea that you tore apart one of the triangular eaves of the carton, pushing its wing flaps back, using the stiffness of its own glued seam against itself, forcing the seal inside out, without ever having to touch it, into a diamond-shaped opening which became an ideal pourer, a *better* pourer than a circular bottle opening or a pitcher's mouth because you could create a very fine stream of milk very simply, letting it bend over that leading corner, something I appreciated as I was perfecting my ability to pour my own glass of milk or make my own bowl of cereal—the radiant idea filled me with jealousy and satisfaction. I have a single memory of a rival cardboard

[1] For example, I feel no loss that doctors don't perform house calls: only one house call was ever paid on me, after I had been hallucinating in a measles fever that the motionless flame of a bedside candle had bent toward me and flowed like some very warm drink along the roof of my mouth, and I was so young when it happened (three, I think) that the black bag with its interesting pair of circular hinges is almost mythological now; certainly not missed: the real beginning point of the history of medicine for me is in doctor's offices, waiting to have shots. Likewise, I don't grieve over the great shift in library checkout procedures that happened in the sixties: instead of a due date stamped on a card that held earlier due dates (allowing you to learn how frequently a particular book had been checked out), the assistant librarian laid out (1) the typed title-card for the book, (2) your own library card, and (3) a computer-punch card that bore a preprinted due date, next to each other within a large gray photographing box, and pressed a worn button; for me the history of libraries begins with the shutter-flashes in that gray box. (Having not seen one in a long time, I may be fusing some details of the gray microfilm reader in with it.)

method, in which a paper stopper was built into one corner of a flat-topped carton; but the triumphant superiority of the peaked-roof idea, which so gracefully uses the means of closure as the means of dispensation (unlike, say, the little metal pourers built into the sides of Domino sugar or Cascade dishwashing detergent boxes, which while intrinsically interesting are unrelated to the glued flaps of cardboard at their tops and bottoms), swept every alternative aside.

But I also had a strong counter-fascination for the system of home delivery, which managed to hold on for years into the age of the paper carton. It was my first glimpse of the social contract. A man opened our front door and left bottles of milk in the foyer, on credit, removing the previous empties—mutual trust! In second grade we were bussed to a dairy, and saw quart glass bottles in rows rising up out of bins of steaming spray on a machine like a showboat paddle as they were washed. Despite my intense admiration for the carton, I felt superior to those who reached into the supermarket's dairy case and withdrew Sealtest products, admitting to the world in doing so that they did not have home delivery and hence were not really members of society but loners and drifters. Yet soon I began to sense that everything was not right in the realm of home delivery. We had begun with Onondaga Dairy, their quart glass bottles topped with a paper cap that held the glass with folded pleats, their trademark an American Indian child wearing the kind of Western-movie feather headband that I doubt was ever worn among the tribes of upstate New York. Then the dairy mergers began. Milk continued to appear without interruption, but the name on the step-van, and the step-van itself, kept changing. Deliveries went from three times to twice a week. Strange, foreign half-gallon bottles—Keen Way Dairy is the only one I remember—began cropping up: one dairy was using the bought-out bottles of other defunct dairies, meaning that *the name molded in the glass no longer matched the name printed on the cap,* a disturbing discordance. Then glass was abandoned altogether, replaced first by white plastic containers with red handles, and then by the very same Sealtest cartons you could buy in the supermarket. Out of habit or a reverence for tradition, we continued to take home delivery, even though the delivered milk often went bad more quickly, after a day in the foyer, unrefrigerated, while my parents worked and my sister and I were at school. Though I resisted it at first, my mother began buying supplemental cartons of Sealtest from the A&P, or sending me out to buy them from the mom-and-pop stores; but in order to keep (we thought) the home-delivering dairy afloat in these twilight years, we responded to the sad promotional leaflets they left between the cartons, diversifying into orange juice, chocolate milk, cottage cheese, buttermilk. By this time the step-van had no name painted on it at all; we were the last house on the street and perhaps in the whole neighborhood still taking deliveries, doubtless more of a nuisance than a mainstay: the delivery man, a different person every other week, would accelerate roughly as soon as he had swung back into the seat and put the van in gear—he had a whole city of isolated sentimentalists to cover. Finally the last merged dairy left a leaflet saying that they were discontinuing home service, and the transition was complete. I'll guess and say that it was 1971. Did I mourn? Any sadness I felt was overpowered by an embarrassment that we had associated ourselves with the losers, services that could be grouped with horse-drawn ice and coal trucks, Fuller brush men, and person-to-person telephone calls, in an age of Brasilia, of Water Piks, of wheeled and segmented arms that telescoped out from airport gates to press their vinyl, curve-accommodating terminus against the riveted door-regions of unloading passenger planes, and of escalators.

But because the whole gradual change was complete before I became an adult, whenever I think over it I am tempted away from history into all kinds of untrustworthy emotional details. It took my mother a few years before she stopped absentmindedly trying to tear open the wrong side of the Sealtest carton, despite my having lectured her on the fact that one triangle was much more heavily glued than the other, their difference indicated by the words "Open Here," enclosed in the outline of an arrow—to disregard it was to fail to take the invention seriously. My father made iced coffee after a morning of lawn-mowing or shrub transplantation, and often he left the carton sitting out on the counter afterward, *with the spout open.* And here I am pulled, willingly by this time, to consider my father's great iced coffee: several spoonfuls of instant coffee and sugar, liquefied into a venomous syrup by a bare quarter-inch of hot tap water to remove any granulation, then four or even five ice cubes, water to halfway up the glass, and milk to the top: so many ice cubes that until they melted a little, hissing and popping, with the milk falling in diffusional swirls around them, he could barely get a spoon to the bottom of the glass to stir the drink.[1] His plan was to market a bottled mocha version of it called Café Olé, a mock-up of which, with a dramatic Zorro-like logo scripted diagonally across the label, sat on our mantel for a while after the plan was set aside. I have to include, too, the subsidized half-pints of milk we bought in school for four cents and raced each other to drink in one skull-chilling continuous inhalation on the paper straw—this mystical four cents linked both with the picture of the tall glass of milk in the poster of the four food groups, and with the rule that you should have four glasses of milk every day, a rule I faithfully followed, drinking four at one sitting just before bed if I had to.

All of these nostalgia-driven memories pour out of that

[1] The ice cube tray deserves a historical note. At first there were aluminum barges inset with a grid of slats linked to a handle like a parking brake—a bad solution; you had to run the grid under warm water before the ice would let go of the metal. I remember seeing these used, but never used them myself. And then suddenly there were plastic and rubber "trays," really molds, of several designs—some producing very small cubes, others producing large squared-off cubes and bathtub-bottomed cubes. There were subtleties that one came to understand over time: for instance, the little notches designed into the inner walls that separated one cell from another allowed the water level to equalize itself: this meant that you could fill the tray by running all the cells quickly under the tap, feeling as if you were playing the harmonica, or you could turn the faucet on very slightly, so that a thin silent stream of water fell in a line from the tap, and hold the tray at an angle, allowing the water to enter a single cell and well from there into adjoining cells one by one, gradually filling the entire tray. The intercellular notches were helpful after the tray was frozen, too; when you had twisted it to free the cubes, you could selectively pull out one cube at a time by hooking a fingernail under the frozen projection that had formed in a notch. If you couldn't catch the edge of a notch-stump because the cell had not been filled to above the notch level, you might have to mask all the cubes except one with your hands and turn the tray over, so that the single cube you needed fell out. Or you could twist all the cubes free and then, as if the tray were a fry pan and you were flipping a pancake, toss them. The cubes would hop as one above their individual homes about a quarter of an inch, and most would fall back in place; but some, the loosest, would loft higher and often land irregularly, leaving one graspable end sticking up—these you used for your drink.

Sealtest carton, pulling me off course, distorting what I want to be a simple statement of gratitude for a great packaging design that happened to come into widespread use when I was little. I look forward to the time when I will have thought about milk and cheese products enough as an adult that the unpasteurized taint of sentimentality will lift from the subject; but so far, aside from the recent cream-cheese-and-sliced-olive thing, only one additional unit of dairy thinking has occurred to me: I have lately turned against milk as a beverage. In my first year of college it became widely believed that "milk makes more mucus" and hence should be avoided when you have a cold—that was the beginning of my disenchantment. I noticed soon afterward that it seemed to coat my tongue and give me bad breath, something I was, as I have said, very anxious to avoid, and then a few years later it developed that L. was allergic to milk: it gave her blood-flecked diarrhea, and the sight of someone swallowing a full cold glass on TV made her moan with distaste. Before she understood that she was physically allergic, she ascribed her dislike to her father's influence: he, she told me, associated dairy products with a certain kind of cheerful brutishness—blond mezzosoprano camp counselors in Wagnerian horn-hats sitting among the lupins drinking bowl after bowl, their knees and cheekbones visibly growing. She remembered his quoting Tacitus's *Germania* darkly, something about "barbarians who buttered their hair." (Or was it not Tacitus but Ammianus Marcellinus?) And I, influenced by her dislike, began to feel uncomfortable when I saw the semi-opaque coating left on the side of a glass of half-drunk milk narrowing up to where someone's lips had slurped at the rim; my pity for all those bouts of diarrhea that she had gone through before she understood her allergy and my own deep desire not to be thought of as a hair-butterer combining. When she had to use milk in a recipe, she would sniff at the open carton suspiciously, uncertain of its freshness, but uncertain too whether her uncertainty was not actually an aversion to its normal smell; and she would finally say, "This seem all right to you?" handing me the carton with a pragmatic, pursed-lip, frowning expression I liked a lot—the "Would you kindly corroborate this bad odor?" expression—studying my face carefully as I put my nose to the carton. And here was another wayside greatness of the milk carton: the small diamond shape of the spout is a perfect fit for the nose, concentrating any scent of sourness: no wide, circular milk-bottle opening could have been nearly as helpful for diagnosis.

I have, then, only one unit of adult thought about milk to weigh against dozens of childhood units. And this is true of many, perhaps most, subjects that are important to me. Will the time ever come when I am not so completely dependent on thoughts I first had in childhood to furnish the feedstock for my comparisons and analogies and sense of the parallel rhythms of microhistory? Will I reach a point where there will be a good chance, I mean a more than fifty-fifty chance, that any random idea popping back into the foreground of my consciousness will be an idea that first came to me when I was an adult, rather than one I had repeatedly as a child? Will the universe of all possible things I could be reminded of ever be mostly an adult universe? I hope so—indeed, if I could locate the precise moment in my past when I conclusively became an adult, a few simple calculations would determine how many years it will be before I reach this new stage of life: the end of the rule of nostalgia, the beginning of my true Majority. And, luckily, I *can* remember the very day that my life as an adult began.

Chapter Seven

IT HAPPENED when I was twenty-three, four months into my job on the mezzanine, at a time when I owned only five shirts. Each of them could be worn, at the most, three times, except for the blue, which continued to look sharp well into the fourth wearing, as long as none of the previous wearings had been on unusually hot days. The cleaner's would accept no fewer than three shirts at a time, and they took four days, so frequently there would be a single shirt hanging in my large, resonant closet when I came home from work.

On that morning of my adulthood, I had on my bureau an unopened brown paper parcel containing three clean shirts. I pried off the string (for it never paid to try to snap the string that early in the morning, or to fiddle with the rapid but excellent dry cleaner's knot), and let string and paper fall at my feet. My mother had sometimes brought home paper parcels of thinly sliced Westphalian ham and allowed me to open them, and this first moment of shirt disclosure had something of the earlier Westphalian unveiling, yet it was perhaps even more pleasing, because in this case I was rediscovering my old buddies, articles of clothing I had worn many times before, now made almost unrecognizably new, no longer wrinkled inside the elbows or around the waist where I had tucked and retucked them, but wrinkled with positive kinds of semi-intentional knife-edge creases and perpendicular fold-lines that only heightened the impression of ironedness, having come about either as a result of the occasionally indiscriminate force of the pressing and starching machines (such as the crow's-feet on the sleeve near the cuffs) or as a result of the final careful foldup. And the shirts weren't merely folded: strips of light blue paper held them tightly and individually to their stored state, their arms impossibly bent behind them as if each were concealing a present.

I looked at the three of them—two whites and the long-running blue—and I decided I would wear my slightly older (four months old) white. Four whole months as a businessman! When I looked closely, I was sure I could detect a slight aging of the cotton—it seemed to be soaking up the starch more completely than the newer white shirt was able to. I snapped the blue paper strip; then I pulled out the shirt cardboard[1] and tossed it on the pile of cardboards I had already saved.[2] I held the chosen shirt in the air with my little finger hooked under the collar and shook it once. It made the sound of a flag at the consulate of a small, rich country. Now—was I ready to put it on?

My T-shirt, of course, was already tucked into my underpants: a few weeks into the job I had discovered that this small act of foresight made the whole rest of the business day much

[1] I used the casual unscabbarding move of retraction I had admired years before in practiced Polaroid owners, who with negligent ease pulled the thick, pre-SX-70 pane of film through rollers that crushed its chemical jellies into a facedown snapshot, and who then walked in little circles, looking at the sky, as they counted chimpanzees to themselves, finally hunching to peel back just the corner, and then more confidently the rest, of the wet, slick black-and-white image, leaving behind a stratiform baklava of trash, composed of the negative set into its baroque casement of multilayered paper, on the back of which you could often find interesting lichen-scapes of green and brown developer seeping through.

[2] Quite a pile by then: I saved them because I had always liked drawing on the shirt cardboards saved from my father's shirts, although his cardboards had been white and glossy on one side and legal-sized, while mine were gray and smaller; also I had found that a shirt cardboard, curved into a trough, made a nice receptacle to hold under your chin as you trimmed your beard, something I had been doing more frequently since starting the job. (At that point, I had not yet rediscovered its usefulness as a dustpan.)

more comfortable. And my suit pants were on but not fastened; I *was* ready. The shirt was always colder than you expected. I began buttoning at the second button from the top, braving the minor pain in my thumb-tip as I pushed that button through and heard the minuscule creaking or winching sound that its edge made in clearing the densely stitched perimeter. From here I progressed right down the central strip of buttons, did up my pants, and moved on to the cuffs. These two cuff buttons were the hardest, because you could use only one hand, and because the starch was always heavier there than elsewhere; but I had gotten so that I could fasten them almost without thinking: you upended the right cuff button with your thumbnail and cracked the starch-fused buttonhole apart over it, closing your fingers hypodermically to propel it into place; then you repeated the procedure with the other cuff. Sped up, the two symmetrical cuff-buttoning sequences would have looked like a Highland reel.

The topmost button called me to the mirror, where I saw my chin jut up into a bulldog expression to make way for the fists at my neck. Then the tie; the belt; the shoes—all automatic subroutines.

I had my coat on when I remembered that I had forgotten to put on antiperspirant. This was a setback. I weighed undoing the belt, untucking the shirt, untucking the T-shirt from the underpants: was it worth it? I was running late.

Here was where I made a discovery. An image came to me—Ingres's portrait of Napoleon. Displacing my tie, I undid a single middle button. Yes, it was possible to get at your underarm by entering the shirt through the gap made by one undone button and then working the stick of antiperspirant up the pleural cavity between T-shirt and shirt until you were able to snag the sleevelet of the T-shirt with a finger and pull it past the seam where your shirtsleeve began, thereby exposing the area you needed to cover. I felt like Balboa or Copernicus. In college I had been amazed to see women take off bras without removing their sweatshirts, by unfastening the rear bra-catch through the material, pushing one sleeve up far enough to slip off one strap, and, after a few arousing shrugs of their shoulders, pulling the whole wriggling thing nonchalantly out of the opposite sleeve. My own antiperspirant discovery had some of the topologically revelatory flavor of those bra removals.[1]

I walked to the subway very pleased with myself. My shoes (very new then; only a few months of wear on the laces) made a nice granular sound on the sidewalks. The subway wasn't crowded, and I got a standing spot I liked, and had room to bend to put my briefcase between my ankles. It was one of those good rides, where the motion of the train is soothing,

[1] The earliest point on this topological time-line, however, came when I was somewhere between three and five years old. I watched my mother select a T-shirt for my sister from a wooden folding structure made of thin dowels over which you draped clothes to dry. The T-shirt happened to have been washed inside out: my mother turned it upside down and reached into the torso of the shirt with one hand, as if fishing for something in a deep bag, and took hold of a sleeve; then she reached in with her other hand and took hold of the other sleeve. She raised her elbows, and the T-shirt began to fall around the two fixed sleeve-points; a last flip and it hung, no longer upside down, *and no longer inside out,* from her fingers. I felt my brain perform an analogous inversion, trying to take in the seeming impossibility and wonderful intelligence of what she had just done. I felt a pang of missed opportunity in not having invented the trick myself—up until then, I had been using pure trial and error to turn my T-shirts right side out: I would push a sleeve in through its hole and get nowhere; tentatively curl the bottom hem back; push the neck partway in and wait for the miracle;—only after several minutes did I get the shirt truly reversed, and it never happened in a way I could later remember. After watching my mother, I practiced her moves until I understood how they worked, repeating, "inside . . . out . . . inside . . . out," as if it were stage patter. I found out, observing a baby-sitter, that other people knew the trick as well; and according to the baby-sitter my mother hadn't taught it to her—rather, the sitter knew it because that was simply the way everyone turned things inside out, all over the city of Rochester. Soon I created a special order in the taxonomy of human dexterity to cover this kind of trick: it was better than being able to whistle, snap your fingers, stand on your head, use the overlapping fly of your underpants without strangling your miniature dick, crack an egg with one hand, or play the *Batman* theme on the piano, because the dexterity was based on a leap of mind that had understood the need for a set of seemingly incomprehensible preparations before a single transforming motion that, like the final flowering of the NBC peacock, disclosed your purpose. I retroactively upgraded shoe-tying into this category, and later included (1) holding a pillow with your chin over the open clean pillowcase, rather than trying to push a corner of the pillow into the retreating flaps of a horizontal pillowcase; (2) placing your coat on the floor, inserting both arms in both armholes, and flipping the coat over your head; (3) forming a simple knot (the base shoe-tying knot) in a string by crossing your arms like Mr. Clean, taking hold of the ends of the string, and uncrossing your arms; (4) pre-bunching the sock before you put it on, though as I have said, I eventually abandoned the practice.

and the interior temperature pleasantly warm but not hot. I imagined the subway car as a rapidly moving loaf of bread. The motto "You can taste it with your eyes" occurred to me. It was a shame, I thought, that white bread had fallen into disfavor, since only white bread looks really good as toast, and only white bread looks good when cut diagonally. I recalled the strange steamy feeling of white toast at the moment you removed it from the toaster—no matter how crumby or disreputable your toaster was, the toast always came out smooth and clean—and the many styles of buttering you could use. You could scrape lightly, keeping to the surface; or if you had colder butter, you might be obliged to crush into the softer layer below the crust as you forced the butter to spread; or you could tap little chips of butter onto the toast without spreading them at all, place the two pieces of toast face to face, and cut them in half diagonally, so that the pressure of the knife stroke aided the melting of the butter in addition to halving the bread. Now, why was diagonal cutting better than cutting straight across? Because the corner of a triangularly cut slice gave you an ideal first bite. In the case of rectangular toast, you had to angle the shape into your mouth, as you angle a big dresser through a hall doorway: you had to catch one corner of your mouth with one corner of the toast and then carefully *turn* the toast, drawing the mouth open with it so that its other edge could clear; only then did you chomp down. Also, with a diagonal slice, most of the tapered bite was situated right up near the front of your mouth, where you wanted it to be as you began to chew; with the rectangular slice, a burdensome fraction was riding out of control high on the dome of the tongue. One subway stop before mine, I concluded that there had been a logic behind the progress away from the parallel and toward the diagonal cut, and that the convention was not, as it might first have appeared, merely an affectation of short-order cooks.

I then began to wonder how late to work I was going to be. My own watch had been stolen by threat of force a week before, but I glanced hopefully down the diminishing perspective of hands and wrists that held the metal loops of the subway car. I spotted many watches, women's and men's, but on this particular morning they were all unreadable. The buckle, and not the face, of one pointed my way; some were too far off; the women's were too small; several lacked all circumferential points of reference, and thus remained Necco wafers to all but their wearers; some were oriented so that glints from their crystals obscured the hands or the diodes beneath. A wristwatch less than a foot from my head, worn by a too carefully shaven man reading a newspaper folded into tiny segments, was exactly half visible; the half I needed was eclipsed by his cuff, so that while I could easily make out the terminal "get" of the tall-lettered trademark, the only time-telling I could do was to determine that it was not yet actually past nine o'clock. The cuff was possibly more expertly starched than my own.

And this was when I realized abruptly that as of that minute (impossible to say exactly which minute), I had finished with whatever large-scale growth I was going to have as a human being, and that I was now permanently arrested at an intermediate stage of personal development. I did not move or flinch or make any outward sign. Actually, once the first shock of raw surprise had passed, the feeling was not unpleasant. I was set: I was the sort of person who said "actually" too much. I was the sort of person who stood in a subway car and thought about buttering toast—buttering raisin toast, even: when the high, crisp scrape of the butter knife is muted by occasional contact with the soft, heat-blimped forms of the raisins, and when if you cut across a raisin, it will sometimes fall right out, still intact though dented, as you lift the slice. I was the sort of person whose biggest discoveries were likely to be tricks to applying toiletries while fully dressed. I was a man, but I was not nearly the magnitude of man I had hoped I might be.

Riding the escalator to street level, I tried to revive the initial pain of the discovery: I had heard a lot about people having episodes of sudden perception like this, and had not undergone many myself. By the time I was outside, I had decided that I had just been through something serious enough that I was justified in taking the time, late or not, to get coffee and a muffin to go at the really good coffee place. Once there, however, as I watched the woman briskly open a small bag for my Styrofoam cup and tissue-protected muffin, using the same loose-wristed flip my mother had used in shaking down a fever thermometer (which is the fastest way to open a bag), and then sprinkle the purchase with handfuls of plastic stirrers, packets of sugar, napkins, and pats of butter, I felt an impatience to get to the office: I looked forward to the morning show-and-tell period with Dave, Sue, Tina, Abe, Steve, and the rest of them, when I would describe, leaning in doorways and on modular dividers, how my personality had ground to an amazing halt, right on the subway, and had left me a brand-new adult. I shot my cuffs and pushed through the revolving door to work.

Chapter Eight

I WAS BOTH RELIEVED and disappointed to find, later, that I wasn't quite so developmentally fixed as it had seemed on that morning; but even so I continued to think of that day as marking a notable, once-in-a-lifetime change of -hoods. Now, keeping this fixed age of twenty-three in mind as the definitive end of my childhood, we'll assume that every day of my life I had thought a constant number of new thoughts. (The thoughts had to be new only to me, previously unthought by me, regardless of whether or not everyone else considered them to be outworn and commonplace; and their actual number was unimportant—one, three, thirty-five, or three hundred a day; it depended on the fineness of the filtration used to distinguish the repeaters from the novelties, as well as on my own rate of new thinking—so long as it remained constant.) We'll assume that all of these new thoughts, once they occurred, did not decompose past a certain point, but rather remained intact to the extent that they could be plucked back into living memory at any later time—even though the particular event, or later new thought, that would remind me of any given earlier thought might never arise. And let's say that my memory began suddenly to function consistently at age six. Under these three simplifying assumptions, I would have laid away in storage seventeen years' worth (23 − 6 = 17) of childish thoughts by the time I finally turned into an adult on that subway ride to work. Therefore, I concluded recently,[1] I needed simply to continue to think more new thoughts at the same daily rate until I passed the age of forty (23 + 17 = 40), and I would finally have amassed enough miscellaneous new mature thoughts to outweigh and outvote all of those childish ones—I would have reached my Majority. It was a moment I had not known existed, but it quickly took on the stature of a great, shimmering goal. It is the moment when I will really understand things; when I will consistently put the past to wise and well-tempered uses; when any subject I call up for mental consideration will have a whole sheaf of addenda dating from my late twenties and my thirties in it, forcing down the primary-

[1] I reached the conclusion as I was driving home fast in the dark, on the highway that only a few days earlier had borne the garbage truck that had reminded me of the railroad spike and the white-background trick. I had been thinking that only after I had become a commuter had I noticed the way cigarette butts, flicked out narrowly opened windows by invisible commuters ahead of me, landed on the cold invisible road and cast out a small firework of tobacco sparks, and how the sight had the same effect on me as the last shot of a scene in *Risky Business:* a late-night Chicago subway train sends off a flare of sparks in the darkness, bringing to a close with a crisp high-hat cymbal "Kssh!" the lulling electronic rhythms of the soundtrack—except that these cigarette sparks were the farewell explosions of such intimate items, still warm from people's lips and lungs, appearing just beyond your headlights and then washed out by them, as you passed the still wildly spinning and tumbling butt that was traveling at forty miles an hour to your sixty-five. This had reminded me of how I used to open the window on car trips when I was little and release an apple or pear core into the bolster of air and noise and watch it shrink away into the perspective of the road behind the car, still bouncing and spinning fast—suddenly changed from something I held in my hand to something not mine that would come to rest on a stretch of highway which had no particular distinguishing feature, a place between human places, as litter; and I was wondering whether the people who tossed their cigarette butts out in the darkness did it simply because they preferred this to stubbing the cigarette out in their ashtray, and because they enjoyed the burst of cold fresh air from the quarter-opened window as they flicked it away, or whether they knew what moments of sublimity they were creating for the nonsmokers behind them, and did it for us—had they noticed those same fireworks trailing other smokers' cars? Did they, with the addict's sentimentality and self-regard, associate this high-speed cremation and ash-scattering with the longer curve of their own life—"Hurled into the darkness in a blaze of glory," etc.? I was turning these various thoughts, some of them new ones and some repeaters, around in my head, when the conclusion arrived.

colored pipings from "when I was eight" or "when I was little" or "when I was in fourth grade," which had been of necessity so prominent. Middle age. *Middle age!*

As I paused for an instant a few feet from the escalators, at the close of my lunch hour on that day my shoelace broke, carrying my Penguin paperback of Aurelius's *Meditations* and my CVS bag, I was two years on my way toward this great goal, though I did not understand it clearly at the time; that is, two-seventeenths, or roughly twelve percent, of the available ideas in my brain at that moment were grown-up ideas, and the rest were childish, and I had to accept them as such.

It happened that nobody was on the escalators just then, either going down or going up, even though the end of lunch hour was a peak time. The absence of passengers, combined with the slight thumping sound the escalators made, quickened my appreciation of this metallic, uplifting machine. Grooved surfaces slid out from underneath the lobby floor and with an almost botanical gradualness segmented themselves into separate steps. As each step arose, it seemed individual and easily distinguished from the others, but after a few feet of escalation, it became difficult to track, because the eye moves in little hops when it is following a slow-moving pattern, and sometimes a hop lands the gaze on a step that is one above or below the one that you had fixed on; you find yourself skipping back down to the early, emergent part of the climb, where things are clearer. It's like trying to follow the curve on a slowly rotating drill bit, or trying to magnify in with your eye to enter the first groove of a record and track the spiral visually as the record turns, getting lost in the gray anfractuosities almost immediately.

Since nobody was on the escalators, I could have played a superstitious game I often played during escalator rides, the object of which was to ride all the way to the top before anyone else stepped onto the escalator behind me or above me. While maintaining the outward appearance of boredom, gliding slowly up the long hypotenuse, I would inside be experiencing a state of near-hysterical excitement similar to what you felt when you were singled out to be chased in a game of tag; the premise, which I believed more and more strongly as I approached the end of the ride, being that if someone got on either escalator before I finished my ride, he or she would short out the circuit, electrocuting me.

I often lost the game, and since once I locked myself into it, it became a somewhat nerve-tingling experience, I was at first relieved to glimpse the head of someone named Bob Leary appearing way up at the top of the down escalator, because his presence made the game an impossibility for the time being. Bob and I had never had one of those less-than-a-minute chats that are sufficient to define acquaintanceship in large companies, yet we knew who the other was, just by having seen the other's name on the distribution lists of memos and on the doors of our offices; a sense of discomfort, or near guilt, was associated with our never having gotten around to performing the minimal social task of introducing ourselves, a discomfort which increased every time we ran into each other. There are always residual people in an office who occupy that category of the not-introduced-to-yet, the not-joked-about-the-weather-with: the residue gets smaller and smaller, and Bob was one of the very last. His face was so familiar that his ongoing status as stranger was really an embarrassment—and just then, the certainty that Bob and I were gradually going to be brought closer and closer to each other, on his down and my up escalator rides, destined to intersect at about the midpoint of our progress, twenty feet in the air in the middle of a huge vaultlike lobby of red marble, where we would have to make eye contact and nod and murmur, or stonily stare into space, or pretend to inspect whatever belongings could plausibly need inspection on an escalator ride, wrenching past that second of forced proximity as if the other person did not exist, and thereby twisting the simple fact that we had never exchanged pleasantries onto an even higher plane of awkwardness, filled me with desperate aversion. I solved the problem by freezing in mid-stride, the instant I caught sight of him (just before I had actually stepped onto the escalator), pointing in the air with an index finger, as if I had just thought of something important that I had forgotten to do, and walking off quickly in another direction.[1]

[1] You can never be sure whether people have noticed this kind of evasion or not. I ran into Bob Leary at the copying machine several weeks after our near encounter—his department's copier was being serviced—and perhaps

I walked quickly through the bank of elevators that handled traffic for the fourteenth through twenty-fourth floors, out into the other side of the lobby, past the long, low building directory, in which white names and floor numbers glowed out of a black background (although little imperfect slits of light were visible in the black film here and there, where a less artful hand had updated the list of tenants), past a grouping of plants I had never noticed before, where a woman in a blue business suit stood paging through a stiff new manila folder that she had pulled from her equally new briefcase.[1] Circling back around to the front of the lobby again, I passed several guys from the mailroom in sunglasses who were lounging on a decorative clump of couches (couches that were really intended for people like the woman with the résumé, and not for support staff from the building to hang out on during lunch break, I thought disapprovingly). I knew them from a time I had had to send a number of last-minute packages via DHL to Padua for a philanthropic thing the company got involved in, so I waved at them. The sound of the mailroom's Pitney Bowes meter machine, which wetted and sealed envelopes in addition to printing a faint red postage emblem on them that included the time, an eagle's wings, and an exhortation to give to the United Way, was loud and rhythmical, and even with

---

in reaction to my cowardice in the lobby, I was booming and hearty and friendly with him, introducing myself and firing up a minute or so of conversation about the decreasing margins in the now mature copying-machine business, and the use of air suction as an element of the paper-feed mechanism that nobody could have foretold. This was all it took: from then on we were perfectly at ease with each other, smiling and nodding when we chanced to see each other in the hall or the men's room—we even worked together briefly on a thirty-page cross-departmental requisition for a fleet of trucks. The ignominy of my having veered away from the escalator that day in order to escape an intersection with him never colored our years of chortliness.

[1]I could guess exactly what she was doing, and the knowledge pleased me. She was going through the copies she had made of her résumé, making sure that the copies that she would casually hand out at anyone's request were not the bad ones with the "New Hapmshire" typo, although she *wasn't* throwing out the "Hapmshire" résumés, but saving them for the interview after the one in this building, in case she didn't have time to revisit a copy center between times, since the second job was one she probably didn't want anyway. I nodded to her in a way that might have been interpreted as patronizing, but was meant to convey fellowship, since I had hung around lobbies with résumés that had typos, wearing a new suit, at one time myself.

earplugs I never would have been able to stand it all day long the way these mailroom guys did. One of them waved back, but before I turned away I was fairly sure that I caught sight of another of them (notable because on hot days, incredibly, this man would wear a clip-on tie clipped to the V at the *second button* of his open-collared shirt, so that the gray plastic stick-figure limbs of the clip-on mechanism were plainly visible) leaning toward the others while looking at me in order to say something mildly malicious about me to them, something like: "A couple of weeks ago, I was walking past that guy's office? I look in: he's right in the middle of pulling a hair from his nose. He goes *doink!* and then he makes a face, *nnng,* eyes watering, and then this *shiver* goes through him. Probably he made a mistake and pulled out three at once." I knew it was some story like that, because I heard "No's!" and laughter at just the right interval after I'd waved to them, and because if I had been lounging on that couch, I would have been tempted to say something mildly malicious about someone like me, too.

Finally I closed in on the escalators again, now viewing them in profile. Bob Leary was gone; several secretaries were riding up. At the base of the machine, though, there now was an interesting little scene. A man from building maintenance, whose name I didn't know, had in my absence wheeled up a cart bearing squirt bottles of various cleaners, spare rolls of toilet paper, brooms, a window-washing squeegee, and lots of other things on it; and as I drew close, he atomized some pale green liquid onto a white bunched-up rag and applied the rag to the rubber handrail of the escalator. He did not make any wiping motions: he simply leaned on the rag with both hands, looking up at one of the secretaries, while the moving handrail polished itself to a blacker gloss. Imagine working in a building where one of the standard weekly jobs of a maintenance person was to polish the handrail of the escalator! The comprehensiveness of this, the all-embracing definition of what a clean office building really was, was thrilling! I was sure that this was one of the parts of the man's job that he liked the most, and not just because it was fun to watch the secretaries, but because it was something that maintenance men had not been doing for hundreds of years: they had been sweeping, repairing damage, mopping, waxing, finding the right key in the large ring that was clipped to a belt loop, but they had only recently begun shining escalator handrails by leaning motionlessly on a white cotton rag, *using* the technology, yet using it so casually that they appeared to us all as if they were lounging against their Camaros at a beach. This guy probably knew every landmark of that rubber handrail as it circled around—the chip in it where it looked as if someone had tried vandalizing it with a knife, and the section where it warped outward, and the little fusion scar where the two ends had been spliced together to close the loop. One of these landmarks was what he no doubt was using to be sure that he held the rag to the handrail long enough to have polished all of it. I said to him, "How's it going?" and then, reminded by the sight of a box of trash bags in the lower tier of his cart, "Ray's out, I hear."

"He came in last week," said the escalator man, "and I told him, 'You're nuts, stay home, all that bending you have to do?' You could see he was hurting. He was holding onto things."

"Awful."

Then, surprisingly, the man shrugged. "He'll be fine. This happened to him once before. It's not serious in my opinion."

"You know Tina, the secretary Tina?" I said, pointing up at the mezzanine.

"I know Tina."

"Tina has made a get-well poster for him, kind of cornball, with flowers, but really nice, a big poster—it's up there if you want to sign it."

"Maybe I'll get up there this afternoon." He lifted the rag that had been pressed to the handrail and looked at its underside. The edges of the random folds were already darkened where they had been in contact with the rubber. He bunched the rag a different way, sprayed it with more polish, and reapplied it. "Definitely I'll sign it. We've got to get Ray healthy so I don't have to run around doing his work."

"Ray was fast," I said.

"He is fast. You have to respect his speed. They've got a kid in to help out but he's no good."

We told each other to take it easy. Then I took hold of the handrail that he had not been polishing (it would have been odd to grasp the handrail he *had* been polishing—like walking on a newly mopped floor: it would have heightened the always nearby sense of the futility of building maintenance—better to wait until the man had finished the whole handrail before I contributed to the inevitable dulling process that would force him to polish it all over again next week), and I stepped onto the escalator. Without having to look down, I was able to time the moment I took the step that put me in contact with the moving grooves of the escalator so that my foot landed not on a crack between two steps, but on the middle of one of them; and even though just about everyone my age has mastered this skill, I still felt proud of myself, just as I had felt proud of being able to tie my shoes without looking. I also knew by habit just how high the still half-formed and growing escalator step would be as my other foot landed on it, in part gauging the speed of the escalator from the feel of the handrail in my hand. One of the things my mother taught me when I was very little (her emphasis on safety due probably to the fact that escalators and unmanned elevators were still somewhat novel then, and therefore were thought to be, like CRT screens and microwave ovens later, full of new dangers) was always to be sure to retie my sneakers before I used any system of vertical transport. The loose shoelace, I was told, could become caught in the crack between two steps, and I imagined the results: the steps begin to flatten themselves for their Trophonian redescent, hauling Struwwelpeter with them, threshing him, shoe, leg, torso, and finally head, through the metal tines at the top of the circuit, and then steamrolling him still further in the hard-to-picture flat journey in the underside of the stairs. (This was long before I had seen escalators taken apart for repairs, as we often see now in subways, where they break down much more frequently than in corporate settings—is it the heat, or bad maintenance schedules, or the amount of water and dirt and chewing gum they have to handle?—and the triangular shape of the steps finally became clear: before that, the subsiding of what I believed to be a rectangular block into a two-dimensional surface at the end, like the folding up of a travel alarm clock, seemed impossibly complicated.) In high school, I used to ride escalators with my shoes left deliberately untied, in order to demonstrate to myself how safe escalators were, how casually they could be treated[1]—this was during a phase in which I allowed my shoes to come untied and didn't bother to retie them, or even slipped them on in the morning untied, as if

[1] And escalators *are* safe: their safety the result (I now believe) of a brilliant decision to groove the surfaces of the stairway so that they mesh perfectly with the teeth of the metal comblike plates at the top and bottom, making it impossible for stray objects, such as coins or shoelace-ends, to get caught in the gap between the moving steps and the fixed floor. I gave no direct thought to the escalator's grooves that afternoon, and indeed at that time I had indistinct notions as to their purpose—I thought they were there for traction, or possibly were purely decorative; grooved to remind us of how beautiful grooved surfaces are as a class: the grooves on the underside of the blue whale that must render some hydrodynamic or thermal advantage; the grooves left by a rake in loose soil or by a harrow in a field; the single groove that a skater's blade makes in the ice; the grooves in socks that allow them to stretch, and in corduroy, down which you can run your ballpoint pen; the grooves of records. During the period that I rode the escalators with untied shoelaces, I spent the winters speed-skating (an escalator step, incidentally, looks like a row of upturned skate blades) around and around an outdoor pond behind old Italian skaters with raisin faces and hooded sweatshirts who held their skate guards behind their backs and moved with long, slow unvarying strokes; and the summers I spent listening to records: twice a week or so, I rode the very short escalator to the second level of the Midtown Plaza Mall, and as the steps of the escalator pulled in their chins at the top, I would get a first shot, directly at eye level, of the stretch of floor that led past the boxlike theft detectors and into the carpeted region of Midtown Records. There, with let-your-fingers-do-the-walking motions, I would leaf through the albums: if there were multiple copies of the same album I got a primitive nickelodeon animation of the artist sitting still at the piano, looking pompous, under the ornate yellow Deutsche Grammophon title bar; often a slight vacuum between the shrink-wrap of one album and the next pulled the succeeding one a few degrees along before it fell back.

Believing firmly in symmetry in those days, I tried to make comparisons between the grooves associated with these two seasonal activities, skating and record-playing. If explorers were lowered into a highly magnified groove left by a speed-skater's blade, one of my own grooves in the ice of Cobb's Hill Pond, for instance, now irrevocably melted, and stood in that immense tilted valley, our beards whitened with condensation, exhausted from the previous two hours of slow traversal, our packs laden with chunks which we had collected for later labwork and which, like small moraine stones that still retain the characteristic parallel scratches left as the weight of a glacier forced other stones slowly past them, might hold markings only my skate blade could have made, we would see dark gleams here and there, among the great crushed, laterally displaced plasticities resulting from the millennium of that single skate stroke, and near them fragile growths that demonstrated what the professors had always maintained—that ice was slippery because it momentarily melted under the pressure of the blade's

they were loafers. There were a few years there when lots of undergraduates walked around with laces untended to—1977 or so, simultaneous with Dr. Scholl's sandals, I think. I had appropriated the practice, thinking it was cool, but my mother,

---

edge, then refroze when the blade was gone, mounding into brittle crystalline shrubbery that evaporated, even as we watched, into a whitish mist. Those dark gleams would prove, as we drew closer and bent to inspect them, to be small sheared pieces of metal—skate-blade wear.

If you made a negative of that image of my skate blade's gorge, you would arrive at the magnified record groove—a hushed black river valley of asphaltic ripples soft enough to be impressed with the treads of your Vibram soles: an image cast from a master mold that was the result of a stylus forced to plow through wax as it negotiated complex mechanical compromises between all the various conceptually independent oscillations that stereophony demanded of it; ripples so interfingered and confused that only after a day with surveying equipment, pacing off distances and making calculations (your feet sparking static with each step), are you able to spray-paint "Bass Clarinet" with some confidence in orange on an intermittent flume of vinyl, as workers in Scotchgard vests spray-paint the road to indicate utility lines beneath. Cobblestone-sized particles of airborne dust, unlucky spores with rinds like coconuts, and big obsidian chunks of cigarette smoke are lodged here and there in the oddly echoless surface, and once in a while, a precious boulder of diamond, shorn somehow from the stylus by this softer surface, shines out from the slope, where it has been pounded deep into the material by later playings, sworn at by the listener as if it too were common dust. That was needle wear.

As in the later case of the frayed shoelace, what I wanted here was tribology: detailed knowledge of the interaction between the surfaces inflicting the wear and the surfaces receiving it. For skating: Were there certain kinds of skate strokes that were particularly to blame for the dulling of the skate blade? The sprinting start, the sideways stop? Was very cold ice, or ice with a surface already crosshatched with the engravings of many other blades, liable to dull my blades faster? Was there a way to infer total miles skated by the wear inflicted on the edge of a blade? And for records: Was it the impurities in the vinyl that wore down the needle, or was it the ripples of vinyl music itself, and if it was the music, could we find out what sorts of timbres and frequencies made for a longer-lived needle?

Or was most of the wear to the stylus in practice incurred before it ever touched the record, by a human thumb? That was a possibility. If my sister had been playing one of our oldest family records, like *My Fair Lady*, which were allowed to rest on the carpet when not in use—were in fact visibly hairy—there would be a blue-gray fez of dust left on the stylus, made apparently of the same material that coats the filter-screen of the clothes dryer and the inner surface of gerbil nests, and this inanimate harvest was mine to whisk away. Great men from Hirsch-Houck Labs, echoed by the owner's pamphlet that had come with the Shure cartridge, strongly advised you never to perform the whisking with your stereo system turned on, because you might cause "transients" that could overtax the powerful and obliging magnets within your speakers; but the risk had to be run, as far as I

who happened to be taking some classes at the time at the University of Rochester, found it affected and irritating and thought I should stop; and now I can certainly understand how the sight of groups of nineteen-year-olds shuffling

---

was concerned, because the act of removal was confirmed only when the growl of your own thumbprint, each groove sonically magnified, filled the room as you ever so gently drew it under the stylus—playing its unique contour-plowed furrows just as you would soon be playing the spiraled record of one unique studio session in the life of a pianist—and *My Fair Lady*'s fuzzball had fallen away, revealing the tiny point of contact itself, curiously blunt, shaped like the rubber mallet used to elicit a motor reflex from the knee, hanging insectivorally there in space, ready for a new Deutsche Grammophon. The album was still sealed; and here you experienced a further sort of groove before playing the actual record: the soundless and perfectly unresistant parting of the album's plastic shrink-wrap as you pierced it with your thumbnail and drew it down the temporary groove (between what you knew to be, although this was not visible beforehand, two separate sides of cardboard), taking a moment to consider the unusual properties of this shrink-wrapping material, so strong and stretchable until locally breached, and then willing to continue the tear almost of its own accord, a characteristic nicely exploited by the designers of cigarette packs, who build into the cellophane a little colored tab that initiates the tear and a guide-band of thicker plastic that shepherds the effortless undoing around the top of the package. You withdrew the record without ever making contact with the musical surfaces, using a tripod grip: thumb at the edge, two fingers in the middle on the label. Though brand-new, the record would have attracted ambient dust in its passage through the air and onto the turntable; hence you used a record-cleaning system such as the one we had: a separate tonearm-like device that held a fan of superfine bristles to the record in front of a red cylindrical brush that caught any bulk debris. This cleaning arm rode the record slightly faster than the real tonearm, drawn ahead possibly by its multiple inner bristle-points of contact (a puzzle I never really solved), and thus it finished about five minutes before the music did on that side. The record-cleaning system was strongly reminiscent of the yellow street-sweeping machines that were introduced in my childhood, with sprayers in front that wetted approaching debris so that circular spinning brushes could hustle it inward from the curb, into a place of invisible turmoil where a huge bristled reverse-roller at the rear flung it up from the street into a receptacle built into the interior of the machine. If only the record-cleaning systems we used could have worked as well as those street-cleaning machines, which left behind a clean wet track, decorated with ringlets of scrub marks at the outside of the swath and straight sweepings in the middle, even when they swung out from the curb to avoid parked cars and then veered back in to reengage, with obvious satisfaction, the baked mud and leaves and bleached litter of the curb. But no record-cleaning system really worked well; and supposedly the antistatic cleaning solution that you dribbled onto the cylindrical dust brush left an unctuous residue in the grooves, smoothing infinitesimal joys out of the sonic reproduction. Still, we used it; we wetted the brush with solution and laid it in place on the spinning record. And then, ignoring the turntable's bothersome hydraulic

around from class to class with the plastic tips of untied Wallabees and Sears work boots clicking against hallway tile, their socked heels occasionally popping right up out of their footwear, would make you shut your eyes for a second at the

---

cuing mechanism, which had you positioning the skittish tonearm high above the spot you wanted it to land on, you braced your hand against the base of the turntable (in a manner similar to my old way of stabilizing my hand against the sneaker's upper while tying it) and used your thumb to exert a slight, trembly upward lift on the cartridge's gull's-wing finger-hook. Counterweights—brushed chrome disks on calibrated screw threads that could be turned precisely to the desired gram weight (and what controversy there was over what the proper weight should be!—some holding that a two-gram handicap would gradually ruin your records; but stern columnists in *Stereo Review* asserting on the other hand that an insufficient load would possibly allow the stylus to hydroplane over loud passages, or to take off like a skier running a mogul on surface irregularities, coming down injuriously hard on the passages that followed)—caused the tonearm to float upward at the slightest thumb-prompting, as if under the dustcover of this machine a special moon's gravity prevailed. You held the cartridge over the smooth outer perimeter of the revolving record; warps made the surface rise and fall, often in a heartbeat rhythm—*fwoom-hoom, fwoom-hoom*—and onto this moving, pliant surface you finally allowed the stylus to establish gentle contact, so that it too now bobbed along with the waves of warpage, producing as it first landed a concussion like the setting down of a heavy trunk on the carpet, followed by an expanding sigh and at least one big pop that reinforced the feeling that you had now entered the microscopic spell of the technology, in which sounds were stored in a form so physically small that even an invisible particle within a thread-thin groove could resound like the crack of a circus whip, during which sigh you settled back on the carpet from your squatting position. And then the music began. After three minutes of intent listening, once the emotion of the microscopy had worn off and the piano had wandered into passages that were less good or less familiar than the opening, I would begin to read the record jacket, and then, later still, would myself wander into the kitchen to make a sandwich and read *Stereo Review*, returning twenty minutes later, near the end of side A, to listen to the technology finish: you rode the last grooves as if on a rickshaw through the crowded Eastern capital of the music, and then all at once, at dusk, you left the gates of the city and stepped into a waiting boat that pulled you swiftly out onto the black and purple waters of the lagoon, toward a flat island in the middle; rapidly and silently you curved over the placid expanse, drawing near the circular island (with its low druidic totem in the middle, possibly calendrical) but never debarking there; now the undertow bore you at a strange fluid speed back toward the teeming shore of the city—colors, perspiration, sleeplessness—and then again back out over the lagoon; the keel bumped first one shore, then the other, and though your vessel moved very fast it seemed to leave only a thin luminous seam in the black surface behind you to mark where the keel had cut. Finally my thumb lifted you up, and you passed high over the continent and disappeared beyond the edge of the flat world.

mindless monkey-doism of the young. Another thing I did even into adulthood was to retie my shoes on the escalator—making it a little challenge: How late in the ride could I successfully tie both shoes without seeming rushed before I arrived at the top?

Given all of these powerful, preexisting connections in my past life between escalators and shoelaces, you would expect that at the moment I boarded the escalator that afternoon, I would have been forcefully reminded of the problem of shoelace wear which had occupied me an hour earlier. But the determinism of reminding often works obscurely; and in this case the subject had already occurred to me and been laid aside in the few minutes I spent in the men's room before lunch: following this recurrence, the subject didn't arise until very recently, as I began to reconstitute the events of that noontime for this opusculum. Even after lunch, back in my office, as I tore open the stapled top of the CVS bag and pulled the bubble pack of new laces out and wove them into my shoes, zigzagging up every other eyelet with one lace-end, as shoe salesmen had shown me, a moment when I should certainly have been reminded of the subject, I was instead preoccupied with whether I should send off four hundred dollars to Chase Visa, or whether that was too big a chunk and would get me in trouble before my next biweekly paycheck, and I should send only two hundred. Just after lunch always seemed to be the time to think about practical things like bills—and I can't help mentioning here the rarefied pleasure that I took in handling my finances back then: especially the pleasure of getting in the mail fat envelopes filled with charge statements and their receipts, the documentary history of that month, dinners out and odd purchases that you would have forgotten completely but for those slips, which nicely resurrect the moment of paying for you: you're there in the restaurant, very full, an entire steak in your stomach, with your beloved darling, smiling and happy, your bottom by this time on fire from the unabsorptivity of the vinyl seat, and you weigh whether or not to ask her help in calculating the tip—sometimes it is better to be the complete man and dash in a generous round sum, other times it is nice to confer with her about the shades between fifteen and twenty-two percent that evening's waiter or waitress deserved—and you experience the pleasure of writing down the tip's amount through several layers of carbon paper, bearing down hard against the little black tray the restaurant has provided to keep its compensation off the tablecloth, and then, once the totaling has been done and double-checked, you sign, more rapidly than you would sign a business letter because it doesn't matter here what character traits people will read into your signature, and because wine makes you sign more fluently: you whip off most of your last name with the sort of accelerating wriggle that a vacuum cleaner cord makes in retracting into its coiled place of storage[1]—this moment of an evening's closure returns to you entire, rightly sized down to something the size of that duplicate receipt, its carbon image less distinct and the name of the restaurant sometimes barely legible, to accord with its fading state in memory.

No, it was before lunch, only a few minutes after I said good-bye to Tina, that I again briefly took up the thread of shoelace theory.

[1] Sometimes it is better to use the pen the restaurant provides, which is usually a cheap stick pen, even when the restaurant is quite fancy; sometimes it is more satisfying to wait with your hand on your own pen in your shirt pocket until the end of a story you are being told, and then, nodding and laughing, remove it from your pocket, hearing the click of its clip as it slips off the shirt pocket's fabric and springs against the barrel, followed by a second click as you bare the ballpoint—these two sounds being like the successively more remote clicks that initiate a long-distance call that you come to associate with the voice of the person who will answer—audible even in loud restaurants, because the burble of voices is of a much lower frequency. And just as your signature is freed into illegibility by the wine, so you imagine that the very ink in the pen adheres more readily to the tiny pores on the surface of the ball because it has been warmed by your body and by the flow of all this conversation. Rarely do pens go dry in restaurants.

Chapter Nine

A SMALL, perhaps not very interesting question has troubled me occasionally: Is a lunch hour defined as beginning just as you enter the men's room on the way to lunch, or just as you exit it? At the end of an earlier chapter, I instinctively said, "I stepped away toward the men's room, and the lunch hour beyond"; and, right or wrong, this was how I saw the transition: the stop at the men's room was of a piece with the morning's work, a chore like the other business chores I was responsible for, and therefore, though it obviously didn't help the company to make more money, it was part of my job in a way that the full hour of sunlight and sidewalks and pure volition was not. What that meant was that my company was as a rule paying me to make six visits a day[1] to the men's

[1] For new-hires, the number of visits can go as high as eight or nine a day, because the corporate bathroom is the one place in the whole office where you understand completely what is expected of you. Other parts of your job are unclear: you have been given a pile of xeroxed documents and files to read; you have tentatively probed the supply cabinet and found that they don't stock the kind of pen you prefer; relative positions of power are not immediately obvious; your office is bare and unwelcoming; you have no nameplate on the door yet, no business cards printed; and you know that the people who are friendliest to you in the first weeks are almost never the people you will end up liking and respecting, yet you can't help but think of them as central figures in the office simply because they have ingratiated themselves, even if others seem to avoid them for reasons you can't yet

room—three in the morning, and three in the afternoon: my work was bounded and segmented by stops in this tiled decompression chamber, in which I adjusted my tie, made sure that my shirt was tucked in, cleared my throat, washed the newsprint from my hands, and urinated onto a cake of strawberry deodorant resting in one of four wall-mounted porcelain gargoyles.

Is there any other spot in the modern office where a comparable level of mechanical ingenuity is so concentrated and on display? Telephone PBX systems, typewriters, and computers are electronically sophisticated and therefore fundamentally uninteresting. The Pitney Bowes licker-and-stamper and the automatic paper-feed mechanism in the high-speed copier are somewhat more interesting because they are combinations of electronic and mechanical invention—but besides date-stampers and the ball bearings in pens and in desk drawers, which exist in isolation, where but in the corporate bathroom do we witness mechanical engineering in such a pure form? Valves that allow a controlled amount of water to rush into a toilet and no more, shapes of porcelain designed so that the turbulence in them forms almost fixed and decorative (yet highly functional) braids and twists that Hopkins would have liked;[1] a little built-in machine that squirts pink liquefied soap with a special additive that gives it a silvery sheen (also used in

---

grasp. But in the men's room, you are a seasoned professional; you let your hand drop casually on the flush handle with as much of an air of careless familiarity as men who have been with the company for years. Once I took a new-hire to lunch, and though he asked not-quite-to-the-point questions as we ate our sandwiches, and nodded without comprehension or comeback at my answers, when we reached the hallway to the men's room, he suddenly made a knowing, one-man-to-another face and said, "I've got to drain the rooster. See you later. Thanks again." I said, "Yip, take it easy," and walked on, even though I too needed to go, for reasons that will become clearer soon.

[1] For instance: "Before going I took a last look at the breakers, wanting to make out how the comb is morselled so fine into string and tassel, as I have lately noticed it to be. I saw big smooth flinty waves, carved and scuppled in shallow grooves, much swelling when the wind freshened, burst on the rocky spurs of the cliff at the little cove and break into bushes of foam. In an enclosure of rocks the peaks of the water romped and wandered and a light crown of tufty scum standing high on the surface kept slowly turning round: chips of it blew off and gadded about without weight in the air." (Gerard Manley Hopkins, *Journal*, August 16, 1873.)

shampoo recipes now, I've noticed) into the curve of your fingers; and the soap-level indicator, a plastic fish-eye directly into the soap tank, that shows the maintenance man (either Ray or the very one who was now polishing the escalator's handrail) whether he must unlock the brushed-steel panel that day and replenish the supply; the beautiful chrome-plated urinal plumbing, a row of four identical states of severe gnarledness, which gives you the impression of walking into a petrochemical plant, with names like Sloan Valve and Delany Flushboy inscribed on their six-sided half-decorative boltlike caps—names that become completely familiar over the course of your employment even though if asked you couldn't come up with them. Here also, in the midst of the surrounding office's papery, dry, carpeted arrangement of in boxes, framed art gallery posters, and horizontal filing cabinets, you confront a very industrial-looking storm drain set right in the floor. And consider the architectural mazelet you must walk in order to arrive in the bathroom proper after going in the door—an enormous improvement over the older double-door system—intended to keep passing eyes from seeing in. It works, too, no matter how close to the hallway wall you walk: I know because I sometimes tried in passing to glance into the women's corporate bathroom when by chance someone was opening the door, wanting even at the age of twenty-five to glimpse the row of sinks and the women leaning over them toward the mirror to adjust their shoulder pads or put on lip gloss, wanting to see a woman drawing her lower lip tight over her lower teeth à la William F. Buckley, Jr., and then, holding the screwed-out stick of gloss motionless, slide the lip from side to side under it and press her mouth together and then moue it outward, because the sight of this in a corporate setting gave an exotic overlay to memories of my beloved darling getting ready for parties:—the arousing skin-smell of her recent shower, the knowledge that she was putting on makeup to be attractive to other people, the sight of her wearing the holy expression that women have only for themselves in mirrors: slightly raised eyebrows, opened throat, very slightly flared nostrils.

This suggestion of domesticity, come to think of it, contributes a characteristic tone to the inventions found in the corporate bathroom: these inventions are grander, more heroic variants of machines central to our life away from work—the sink, soap dish, mirror, and toilet of home bathrooms. In home bathrooms, the toilet seats are complete ovals, while in corporate bathrooms the seats are horseshoe-shaped; I suppose the gap lessens the problem of low-energy drops of urine falling on the seat when some scofflaw thoughtlessly goes standing up without first lifting the seat. There may be several other reasons for the horseshoe shape, having to do with accessibility, I'm not sure. But I am pleased that someone gave this subject thought, adapting what his company manufactured to deal with the realities of actual behavior. (Until I learned how to raise the seat with my shoe I myself sometimes urinated into toilets with the seat down, and because I am tall, I almost always was inaccurate.) Unlike home rolls, the toilet paper here was housed in a locked device that paid out the frames of paper with a certain amount of resistance, so that you had to pull slowly and carefully in order to keep the paper from tearing on one of the perforations,[1] discouraging waste, and when one roll was spent, a second dropped into place. I was willing to have my wastefulness discouraged, to some degree—before that invention, I had sometimes felt a qualm

[1] Perforation! Shout it out! The deliberate punctuated weakening of paper and cardboard so that it will tear along an intended path, leaving a row of fine-haired white pills or tuftlets on each new edge! It is a staggering conception, showing an age-transforming feel for the unique properties of pulped wood fiber. Yet do we have national holidays to celebrate its development? Are festschrift volumes published honoring the dead greats in the field? People watch the news every night like robots, thinking they are learning about their lives, never paying attention to the far more immediate developments that arrive unreported, on the zip-lock perforated top of the ice cream carton, in reply coupons bound in magazines and on the "Please Return This Portion" edging of bill stubs, on sheets of postage stamps and sheets of Publishers Clearing House magazine stamps, on paper towels, in rolls of plastic bags for produce at the supermarket, in strips of hanging file-folder labels. The lines dividing one year from another in your past are perforated, and the mental sensation of detaching a period of your life for closer scrutiny resembles the reluctant guided tearing of a perforated seam. The only educational aspect of the Ginn series of grade-school readers was the perforated tear-out pages in their workbooks: after you tore out the page (folding it back and forth over the line first to ready it for its rending), a little flap was left bound in the workbook that told the teacher in tiny sideways type what that page was meant to teach the student; the page I remember from first grade was a picture of Jack standing with a red wagon at the top left, and

when I was able to make the roll trundle momentumously around the spindle, reeling off a great drape of unnecessary paper; although when you have a cold and you want a mass of absorbency to hold to your face when you blow your nose, the care you have to take tugging at the nearly tearing paper can be irksome.

Our mezzanine men's corporate bathroom was down a short hallway that housed a recessed row of vending machines and a bulletin board with internal job postings neatly tacked behind glass. In this hallway you could hear the ghostly activity of inaccessible elevator cars as they dropped or rose past our floor—inaccessible because, except for a freight elevator and the emergency stairs, the mezzanine was served only by the escalators. (Besides the offices of three departments of our company, the mezzanine held a restaurant and the offices of a small, once famous mutual fund.) You heard the moans of vertical tradewinds in the elevator shafts, and the clinking of what seemed to be very heavy sets of chains, anchor gauge, possibly safety chains, sinking in heaps onto a basement concrete pad as the cars answered their call buttons. It was a pleasure to consider these boxes of human beings undergoing substantial accelerations somewhere very near me, suspended from bundled filaments of steel, behind one of the hallway

---

Spot waiting for him on the lower right, with a dotted line in a large Z shape connecting the two. The instructions were "Make Jack take the wagon to Spot," or something like that—and you clearly were not supposed to take the direct diagonal route, but rather were meant to travel this pointless Z with your crayon. The sideways explanation on the grown-up side of the perforation claimed that the Z path taught the child the ideal motion of the reading eyeballs—one line of type, a zag of a carriage return, another line of type. I scorned the exercise only a little, because the dotted line itself was like the dotted line printed over perforations in reply coupons and intrinsically beautiful, despite the boy and dog at either end. I was taught, later, about the Indians of New York State, about the making of the Erie Canal, about Harriet Tubman and George Washington Carver and Susan B. Anthony—why don't I have any clear idea even now, after years of schooling, how the perforation of the reply coupon or the roll of toilet paper is accomplished? My guesses are pitiable! Circular pizza cutters with diamond-tipped radii? Zirconium templates, fatally sharp to the touch, stamping the paper with their barbed braillery? Why isn't the pioneer of perforation chiseled into the façades of libraries, along with Locke, Franklin, and the standard bunch of French Encyclopedists? *They* would have loved him! They would have devoted a whole page of beautifully engraved illustration, with "fig. 1's" and "fig. 2's," to the art.

walls, without my knowing architecturally just where they were. Some of the elevator cars were filled with passengers; in others, I imagined, a single person stood, in a unique moment of true privacy—truer, in fact, than the privacy you get in the stall of a corporate bathroom because you can speak loudly and sing and not be overheard. L. told me once that sometimes when she found herself alone in an elevator she would pull her skirt over her head. I know that in solo elevator rides I have pretended to walk like a windup toy into the walls; I have pretended to rip a latex disguise off of my face, making cries of agony; I have pointed at an imaginary person and said, "Hey pal, I'll slap that goiter of yours right off, now I said *watch it!*" The indicator light and slowdown give you enough warning to adjust your glasses and reassume a hieroglyphic expression before other passengers get on. Such moments of privacy were impossible on escalators, but even so I preferred the fairly unusual distinction of reaching my office via escalator over being forced to participate day after day in all the little ceremonies of elevator behavior—raising your eyes with everyone in the car to watch the floor numbers change; assuming the responsibility of holding the "Door Open" button or the rubber door-sensor with a pious expression as people boarded; hearing the tail ends of conversations suddenly become conspiratorial and arch because they are so completely overheard in the press of the car, though they were perfectly commonplace out in the noise of the lobby; interrupting the light beam between the open doors with your hand if nobody gets off or on at a certain floor, to simulate a passing passenger, shortening the wait time; change-jingling; greeting strangers with a voiceless lip-pop made by opening your mouth and then closing it. I did like touching the Braille numbers next to the buttons, and reading the much-xeroxed inspection form, and I liked when the doors began to open just before you had come to a stop so that you could admire the precision of the car's automatic match to the edge of the desired floor; finally, I enjoyed imagining the massive, nimble counterweights scooting roachlike on little three-inch wheels up and down the elevator shaft's rear wall in the opposite direction to the cars.

On this mezzanine hallway, in any case, the impressive row

of vending machines took the place of the bank of elevator doors. I paid no attention to them as I passed, though they deserved attention, and indeed, late most afternoons, when I stopped here (normally on the way back from my fifth company-paid visit to the men's room) to get a snack, I often had inconclusive, repetitive, short-lived thoughts about one or more of them. They seemed in a way like miniature office buildings themselves, except that the descending foodstuffs, unlike life-sized elevator cars, never made stops at intermediate floors, but fell when summoned straight down to lobbies and foyers of varying design. The most elevator-like of all the machines was the one I used the most: it had a panel with three small doors. When you made your selection, a frosted row of metal rungs behind one of the small doors would shift one rung upward (I think it was upward, not downward) and stop, revealing the end of an ice cream bar neatly wrapped in paper. Next to it was a Pepsi machine that often had notes on it saying things like, "This machine ate three quarters of mine!—S. Hollister x7892." And next to the Pepsi machine was a shorter cigarette machine, a holdover from the first great epoch of vending machines, unelectrified, making no change, functioning entirely with the aid of gravity and springs,[1] made by National Vendors of St. Louis. It had two tiers of eleven clear plastic knobs (why *eleven*?); these you pulled on, exerting a satisfying level of force, harder than you used in launching a pinball or playing Foosball, for instance, and it had a wide metal mouth where the chosen brand would slide partially into view. To the right of this machine was a design that resembled the classic 1950s outward-and-upward-angling fast-food/gas-pump style, though it was probably manufactured around 1970 (vending machines, like staplers, are not in the forefront of general stylistic shifts): it was a hot-coffee, tea,

[1] Just as it had in the days when my mother would let me buy her packs of Kents from a machine in the basement of my father's office building, back when heroic French horns helped the Marlboro Man ride across aerial shots of western lands, and when another man toured the magnified minimalist interior of a cigarette butt (I think it was *True,* or one of those single-syllable brands) with a blackboard pointer, showing the TV viewer the features of its proprietary system of Dr. Caligarian baffles, designed by a woman gynecologist, that forced the smoke to leave behind some of its more adhesive resins on the irregular planes of this filter.

and chicken-soup machine, decorated with a backlit white plastic panel that said, "Hot Beverages," in left-handed jaunty *Highlights for Children* handwriting, showing coffee beans spilling from a bean-scooper and an anachronistic china cup and saucer just behind it (such as you would never find in the workplace, except possibly at the officer level or in legal or classy sales settings) giving off a curlicue of steam.[1]

The last vending machine before the doors to the restrooms

[1] I think that in later versions of this model that I saw elsewhere, the overdainty background coffee cup in the backlit panel gave way to a larger, cozier-looking brown ceramic mug, as cups and saucers became alien objects in our lives, brought out in uncomfortable clinky silence on trays only at the end of dutiful dinner parties (following a crashing of pans behind the swinging door to the kitchen, caused by the search for the tray). The motleyness of mugs gradually has taken over because, I assume, mugs simply hold more stimulant, and their larger handles allow a pluralism of grasps—for instance, the two, sometimes three fingers around the handle (cups allow only one finger); or the very common one finger hooking the handle and the thumb and other fingers tripoded onto the body of the mug; or the two-palm grip, ignoring the handle completely, that actresses use when they are playing people having real-life conversations at the kitchen table. The cup forced a primness and feyness to the hand and even caused some pain to the joint of the middle finger which at other times shouldered a pen or pencil, because of the exaggerated distance between the cup's handle and the central weight of the liquid it was supporting. Also, mugs, like car bumpers and T-shirts, have become places for people to proclaim allegiances, names, hobbies, heroes, graphic tastes. Since as a rule you have only one of any particular novelty mug, as opposed to a whole arbor of identical cups hanging from hooks in a white Rubbermaid shelf organizer, you develop a fondness for each mug as an individual, and you try to give even the ones you like least a chance to contain your coffee once in a while—you feel about ugly mugs that you have been given the way you do about bad book-cover designs on paperbacks whose insides you really like—you begin to cherish that slight grit of ugliness and wrongness. Right now, half an hour before I have to leave for work, day before yesterday's mug is on the windowsill still: a really nice white straight-sided spare mug made by Trend Pacific of Los Angeles circa 1982, and decorated with a pattern of thirty identical 1950s kitchen blenders whose electrical cords have round wall-plugs: my question to the talented visionaries at Trend Pacific being, why did they have to wait until appliance plugs had changed from round to square, and blenders had become, *like their avant-garde mug,* spare white creations made by Braun and Krups, before they could illustrate the old golden-agey cartoonish kind of blender? Why do these images have to age before we can be fond of them? But I like this mug in a way I could never like a teacup that was part of a set: it is stylish-looking and I reach for it often when deciding which will be my mug for the morning, despite a theoretical disapproval of camp that I feel able to allude to here probably only because camp, though it is still trickling down through the class structure level by level, has long been

was a recent acquisition. This venturesome snack palace—designed in the era of the Centre Pompidou and of various atriums and malls in which the admittedly beautiful HVAC tubes, huge ribbed versions of vacuum-cleaner or clothes-dryer exhaust tubes, were treated architecturally as ornament—flaunted its interior mechanisms, displaying its inventory behind glass on metallic spirals that turned when you entered the appropriate two-character letter-number combination on a small keyboard. Where old candy machines (similar to cigarette machines—knobbed) might have offered you eight choices, plus a side buffet of chewing gums, this new machine offered *thirty-five* choices, including hard-to-vend bags of chips or pretzels. Your purchase, screwed out into space by the forwarding spiral, fell a fair distance into a low black gulley—hence the pillowy bags of chips were placed into the highest spirals, since they would suffer less damage than, say, a package of Lorna Doones or cheese-and-peanut-butter crackers if dropped from that height; although, oddly, I think I have seen (and bought) granola bars residing in the very top left spiral! The machine had two difficulties, in my experience. (1) The black triangular guard you had to reach past in order to remove your snack from the gulley was excessively heavy and clumsy and powerfully sprung, possibly to discourage pilferage with bent coat hangers, and almost demanded that you use two hands—one to hold the guard open, and one to grasp the Lorna Doones—when very often you had only one hand available, having decided that you wanted a packet of Lorna

---

superseded and in the limbo of its demotions can be glibly disparaged. Of course, though the "serving suggestion" panel on the Hot Beverages vending machine showed a china cup or a mug, in reality the machine dispensed neither for thirty-five cents. The coffee sprayed into a smallish cardboard receptacle without a handle of any kind, not even the ingenious fold-out cantilevered paper handles that seem in general to be vanishing as insulative Styrofoam has moved into dominance, outside of delicatessens. And you might ask, why did a paper cup and not the cheaper, more modern Styrofoam cup drop from inside this vending machine? The answer I came up with, when this question occurred to me in the afternoons, as I stood waiting for the sign saying "Brewing" to go off, was that Styrofoam cups would be too light and clingy to slide down the internal guide-rails into place properly under the spigot—and Styrofoam sticks together: the machine might have a hard time separating one cup from the stack. The cardboard of these cups became almost intolerably hot, and you had to walk very carefully, holding the cup by its cooler rim but avoiding any jostle.

Doones after you had brewed up some thirty-five-cent coffee at the Hot Beverages machine next door; and as a result, gripping a precariously full and hot container of coffee by its rim, with no surface in the area except the floor to rest it on, you were forced to hold open the edge of the black guard with the unpadded bones and tendons of the back of your hand, seize the Lorna Doones, and then withdraw your hand, marveling in the midst of your discomfort that the veins that diagonally crossed those bones and tendons weren't abraded or their flimsy adventitia crushed as that heavy rounded plastic edge was drawn over them. And (2) the spiral invention, though elegant, wasn't infallible: often your last fifty-five cents bought a bag of pretzels that remained hung by one heat-crimped corner out over the drop; nor was there any way to tilt or shake so massive a machine. The next person would get a bonus bag, as the spiral edged yours off with his own.

I didn't think about the vending machines as I passed them, but I did acknowledge their presence in some grateful part of my consciousness, a part equivalent in function to the person in movie credits charged with "continuity," who makes sure that if an actor is wearing a Band-Aid and sitting in front of three pancakes on one day of shooting, the pancakes and the Band-Aid look exactly the same the next day. I depended on the machines' presence as you depend on a certain bulbously clipped corner hedge, or a certain faded poster in the window of the dry cleaner's, as visual nourishment along the way home. And when two years later I walked down that hall and discovered that the cigarette machine—the primary trunk of original innovation from which all the rest of vendition had branched, closely allied with the clinking Newtonianism of the gumball machine and the parking meter—had been replaced by another huge heterodox box that sold yogurt, boxes of cranberry juice, tuna sandwiches, and whole apples, all rotating on a multitiered central carousel accessed through individual plastic doorlets (in compliance with a much-discussed three-phase plan intended to make my company a "smoke-free environment"), I grieved piecemeal over the loss once a day for about a week.

Chapter Ten

FROM THE MEN'S ROOM came the roar of a flushed urinal, followed immediately by "I'm a Yankee Doodle Dandy" whistled with infectious cheerfulness and lots of rococo tricks—most notably the difficult yodel-trill technique, used here on the "ee" of "dandy," in which the whistler gets his lips to flip the sound binarily between the base tone and a higher pitch that is I think somewhere between a major third and a perfect fourth above it (why it is not a true harmonic but rather perceptibly out of tune has puzzled me often—something to do with the physics of pursed lips?): a display of virtuosity forgivable only in the men's room, and not, as some of the salesmen seemed to think, in the relative silence of working areas, where people froze, hate exuding from suspended Razor Points, as the whistler passed. Tunes sometimes lived all day in the men's room, sustained by successive users, or remembered by a previous user as soon as he reentered the tiled liveness of the room. Once, hopped-up after several cups of coffee, I loudly whistled the bouncy opening of the tune that starts out, "All I want is a room somewhere," and then stopped, embarrassed, because I realized that I had unknowingly interrupted someone else's quieter and more masterly whistling of a soft-rock standard with my toneless, aerated tweets; later that day, though, I heard a stylishly embellished version of my tune whistled at the copying machine by someone who must have been in one of the stalls during my earlier roughshod interruption of the soft-rocker.

I leaned quite hard into the men's room door to open it, startling the Doodle Dandy man, who was on his way out, and who turned out to be Alan Pilna from International Service Marketing—his face, when the opening door revealed it, was not formed in the fruity whistler's pout, but had a momentary flinch of surprise on it.

He said, "Oop!"

I said, "Oop!" and then, as he stood aside, holding the door for me to enter, "Thanks, Alan."[1]

I negotiated the quick right and left that brought me into the brightness and warmth of the bathroom. It was decorated in two tones of tile, hybrid colors I didn't know the names for, and the sinks' counter and the dividers between urinals and between stalls were of red lobby-marble. I checked in the mirror to be sure that while chatting with Tina I had not had some humiliating nose problem or newsprint smudge on my face—she would probably have told me about the smudge, but not about the nose. A few sinks over from me, a vice-president named Les Guster was brushing his teeth. He was staring straight at the mirror and very likely seeing there the same expression on his face, the same quick bulgings in his cheek, that he had seen while brushing his teeth since he was eight years old. He blinked frequently, each blink slightly more deliberate than a blink he would have performed while reading or talking on the phone, possibly because the large motor movements of tooth brushing interfered with the autonomic rhythms of blinking. His tap was running. As soon as I took my place at a sink, Les bowed close to his sink, holding his tie with his free hand against his stomach, even though he was clearly not ready to rinse or spit yet, in order to shield his sense of privacy against my presence in the mirror. We were not obliged to greet each other: the noise of the water from his

[1] Among average men, the singular, "oop," is the normal usage; the word is found in its plural as "oops" most often among women, gay men, or men talking to women, in my experience, although there are so many exceptions to this that it is irresponsible of me to bring it up.

tap, and Alan Pilna's winding-down urinal-flush, defined us as existing in separate realms. I was impressed by people like Les who had the bravery to brush their teeth (*before* lunch, even!) at work, since the act was so powerfully unbusinesslike; to indicate to him that I didn't think that his toothbrushing was in any way notable or comic, and that in fact I was unaware of his presence, I leaned into the mirror, pretending to study a defect on my face; then I cleared my throat so unpleasantly that there could be no doubt that I was oblivious to him. I pivoted and stationed myself at a urinal.

I was just on the point of relaxing into a state of urination when two things happened. Don Vanci swept into position two urinals over from me, and then, a moment later, Les Guster turned off his tap. In the sudden quiet you could hear a wide variety of sounds coming from the stalls: long, dejected, exhausted sighs; manipulations of toilet paper; newspapers folded and batted into place; and of course the utterly carefree noise of the main activity: mind-boggling pressurized spatterings followed by sudden urgent farts that sounded like air blown over the mouth of a beer bottle.[1] The problem for me, a familiar problem, was that in this relative silence Don Vanci would hear the exact moment I began to urinate. More important, the fact that I *had not yet begun* to urinate was known to

[1] The absence of stealth or shame that men, colleagues of mine, displayed about their misfortunes in the toilet stall had been an unexpected surprise of business life. I admired their forthrightness, in a way; and perhaps in fifteen years I too would be spending twenty-minute stretches in similar corporate stalls, making sounds that I had once believed were made only by people in the extremity of the flu or by bums beyond caring in urban library bathrooms. But for now, I used the stalls as little as possible, never really at ease reading the sports section left there by an earlier occupant, not happy about the prewarmed seat. One time, while I was locked behind a stall, I did unintentionally interrupt the conversation between a member of senior management and an important visitor with a loud curt fart like the rap of a bongo drum. The two paused momentarily; and then recovered without dropping a stitch—"Oh, she is a very, very capable young woman, I'm quite clear on that." "She is a sponge, a sponge, she soaks up information everywhere she goes." "She really is. And she's tough, that's the thing. She's got armor." "She's a major asset to us." Etc. Unfortunately, the grotesque intrusion of my fart struck me as funny, and I sat on the toilet containing my laughter with the back of my palate—this pressure of containment forced a further, smaller fart. Silently I pounded my knee, squinting and maroon-colored from suppressed hysteria.

him as well. I had been standing at the urinal when he walked into the bathroom—I should be fully in progress by now. What was my problem? Was I so timid that I was unable to take a simple piss two urinals down from another person? We stood there in the intermittent quiet, unforthcoming. Though we knew each other well, we said nothing. And then, just as I knew would happen, I heard Don Vanci begin to urinate forcefully.

My problem intensified. I began to blush. Others did not seem to have any trouble relaxing their uriniferous tubing in corporate bathrooms. Some were obviously so at ease that they could continue conversations side by side. But until I developed my technique of pretending to urinate on the other person's head, the barren seconds I spent staring at the word "Eljer" and waiting for something I knew was not going to happen were truly horrible: even at times when I needed to go badly, if someone else was there, my bladder's cargo would stay locked away behind scared and stubborn little muscles. I would pretend to finish, clear my throat, zip my fly, and walk out, hating myself, sure that the other person was thinking, as his porcelain resounded from his own coursing toxins, "Wait, I don't think I heard that guy actually going! I think he stood there for a minute, *faked* that he had taken a piss, and then flushed and took off! How very weird! *That guy has a problem.*" Later, I would sneak back in, painful with need, and crouch in a toilet stall (so that my head wasn't visible) to urinate without risk. This happened about forty-five times—until one night in the very busy bathroom of a movie theater at the end of the movie, I discovered the trick. When someone takes his position next to you, and you hear his nose breathing and you sense his proven ability to urinate time after time in public, and at the same time you feel your own muscles closing on themselves as hermit crabs pull into their shells, imagine yourself turning and dispassionately urinating onto the side of his head. Imagine your voluminous stream making fleeting parts in his hair, like the parts that appear in the grass of a lawn when you try to water it with a too-pressurized nozzle-setting. Imagine drawing an X over his face; watch him fending the spray off with his arm, puffing and spluttering to keep it from getting in his mouth; and his protestations: "Excuse me?

What are you doing? Hey! Pff, pff, pff." It always worked. If I found myself in very difficult circumstances—flanked on both sides by colleagues, both of whom said hello to me and then began confidently to go—I might have to sharpen the image slightly, imagining myself urinating directly into one of their shock-widened eyeballs.

And now, as the silence lengthened, I resorted to this technique with Don Vanci. After a short mechanical delay, a thick, world-conquering rope of ammonia sprung onto the white slope of porcelain. I gave it a secondary boost from my diaphragm, and it blasted out. Don Vanci and I finished at about the same time; turning from the urinals, just before we flushed in near unison, we greeted each other:

"Don."

"Howie."

Les Guster was on his way out, his toothbrush stowed in a plastic ribbed travel container. He nodded at us. "Gentlemen."

Don Vanci followed Les Guster out without washing his hands.

Chapter Eleven

UNTIL SOMEONE EMERGED from the stalls, I had all four sinks to myself; I chose the one that wasn't surrounded by pools of water. I set down my paperback and rested my glasses on it; then I washed my hands briefly, making the date I had stamped on my palm fade but not disappear. Without turning off the water, I used a paper towel to dry my hands. We had the finest style of paper-towel dispenser available, I think. It was a kind you saw frequently in corporate bathrooms: a six- or seven-foot-high architectural element, a band of brushed steel, laid almost flush with the wall, into which was recessed a diamond-shaped opening that offered you the next paper towel, and, just below it, a waste region where you could throw the towel away. The maintenance man unlocked the front panel of this unit—perhaps using the very same key that opened the soap dispenser, or perhaps not—emptied the trash bag full of used paper towels, and loaded hundreds of just-unbound and slowly expanding new towels into a queue above the diamond cutout. The paper towels themselves were the best kind: nearly a foot wide, wavily embossed, white, folded with two flaps for easy removal—it was an honor to use them. Since the cost of paper has gone up so much in the last decade, some companies that used to use these wide towels have installed an adapter in the dispenser that allows it to handle smaller, cheaper ones. Other facilities managers have turned even more radical, installing, *right beside* the ghost town of the brushed-steel dispenser, a plastic Towlsaver with a little lever like a slot machine's that you have to pull four times, advancing a large internal roll, before you get an acceptable, crumplable length of brown rough paper, which you tear off against a set of metal teeth with a satisfying sound. Another version of this replacement machine has a rotating crank with a calculatedly low gear ratio: they hope that you will tire of cranking sooner, and use less paper. At the very bottom of the range, though it once (to me as a child, at least) was an exciting symbol of futurismo progress, is the "hazards of disease" machine—the hot-air blower. You find it now not only in thruway rest stops, but in the restrooms of Friendly's, Wendy's, Howard Johnson's, and other great chains. What they seem to have done, at least for a short period—the well-meaning but deluded managers responsible for overseeing bathroom cost-control in these chains, I mean, hypnotized by the sales rap of hot-air blower companies—was to rip out their paper-towel dispensers, bolt lots of hot-air blowers on the walls, and then *remove all the wastebaskets.* Towels were what filled the wastebaskets; the restaurants no longer provided towels; therefore they no longer needed to pay bodies to empty the wastebaskets. But in removing that wastebasket, they removed the only unpostponable reason for a staff member to glance over the bathroom at least once a shift, and the place quickly became a wasteland. Meanwhile, are people truly content to be using the hot-air blower? You hit the mushroom of metal that turns it on and, as the instructions recommend, you Rub Hands Gently under the dry blast. But to dry them even as thoroughly as a single paper towel would dry them in four seconds, you must supplicate under the droning funnel for thirty seconds, much longer than anyone has patience for; inevitably you exit flicking water from your fingers, while the blower continues to heat the room. In case you do decide to stand for the full count, the manufacturer (World Dryer Corporation) has provided a short silk-screened text to read to pass the time. I disapprove of this text now, but when I was little it bespoke the awesome oracular intentionality of prophets whose courage and confidence allowed them to scrap the old ways and start fresh: urban renewal architects; engineers of traffic flow; foretellers of monorails, paper clothing, food in capsule form, programmed learning, and domes over Hong Kong and Manhattan. I used to read it to myself as if I were reciting a quatrain from the *Rubáiyát*, and I read it so many times that now it holds for me some of the Ur-resonances of Crest's "conscientiously applied program of oral hygiene and regular professional care." It says:

> To Serve you better – – – We have installed Pollution-Free Warm Air Hand Dryers to protect you from the hazards of disease which may be transmitted by towel litter,
> This quick sanitary method dries hands more thoroughly prevents chapping – – – and keeps washrooms free of towel waste.

In the corner of this statement, World has printed the small Greek letter that looks like a hamburger in profile, the symbol of the environmental movement, a symbol that in seventh grade I cut out of green felt and glued to five white felt armlets, which four friends and I wore when we went out with trash bags and picked up litter on Milburn Street near the school (finding surprisingly little, and feeling the hugeness of the city, litter-filled, around us) on the first Earth Day celebration, whenever that was—1970 or 1971. But does the environmental movement have anything to do with the reason why the Wendy's restaurant that I stood in on September 30, 1987 (copying the legend out, while I counted at MM=60 to be sure that the warm air really did blow for about thirty seconds as I had estimated) had installed this machine in its men's room? No. Is it, in fact, an efficient, environmentally upright user of the electricity produced by burning fossil fuels? No—there is no off button that would allow you to curtail the thirty-second dry time—you are forced to participate in waste. Does it prevent chapping? *Dry air?* Is it quick? It is slow. Is it more thorough? It is less thorough. Does it protect us from the hazards of disease? You will catch a cold quicker from the warm metal public dome you press to start the blower than from plucking a sterile piece of paper that no human has ever held from a towel dispenser, clasping it in your very own hands to dry them, and throwing it away. Come to your senses, World! The tone of authority and public-spiritedness that surrounds these falsehoods is outrageous! How can you let your marketing men continue to make claims that sound like the 1890s ads for patent medicines or electroactive copper wrist bracelets that are printed on the Formica on the tables at Wendy's? You are selling a hot-air machine that works well and lasts for decades: a simple, possibly justifiable means for the fast-food chains to save money on paper products. Say that or say nothing.

But far more important than silk-screened hype is the fact that in trading paper towels for this blower, with its immovable funnel, the food chains, aided by World's rhetoric, are pretending that the only thing you do with paper towels is dry your hands. Not so, not so! You need paper towels to dab at a splash of food on your sleeve that you notice in the mirror; you need them to polish your glasses dry; you need them to wash your face. When you are oily-faced on a hot afternoon in a room made hotter by the hot-air dryer and you decide you want to wash your face before you order your Big Classic, what do you do? Out of desperation, real and true desperation that I myself have experienced, you resort to the toilet paper. So much toilet paper is being used in bathrooms with hot-air blowers that some of the same facilities managers who thought they were cost-cuttingly crafty in moving to blowers have gone to the opposite extreme in the area of toilet-paper dispensers, installing gigantic side-mounted hundred-thousand-sheet rolls the size of automobile tires in each stall. But even so, toilet paper is ill suited to functions outside of a narrow range of activities. You go into a stall and pull yourself a huge handful (that's assuming that the stall is untenanted), and return to the sink with it. As soon as you dampen it with warm water, it wilts to a semitransparent puree in your fingers. You move this dripping plasma over your face; little pieces of it adhere to your cheek or brow; then you must assemble another big wad to dry off with—but ah! now your fingers are wet, so that when you try to pull more toilet paper from the hundred-thousand-sheet roll, the leading end simply dissolves in your fingers, tearing prematurely. Deciding to let your face air-dry, you look around for a place to throw out the initial macerated flapjack, and discover that the wastebasket is gone. So you drop it in the corner with the other miscellaneous trash, or flip it vengefully in the already clogged toilet.

And that is why I considered it an honor to be working at a place that still used the classic corporate paper-towel dispenser. But sometimes when I pulled several paper towels from it, or when I opened a gray steel supply cabinet stocked with black-handled scissors, Page-A-Day calendar refills, magnetized paper-clip dispensers, staplers, cobra-like staple removers, and box after box of Razor Point pens, or when I got a memo with a distribution cover sheet that had fifty names on it, I would suddenly start to doubt that the company I worked for could afford all this. I would think of the people in my department, one department out of maybe sixty-five in the corporation: I would visualize my salary, plus Tina's, Abelardo's, Sue's, Dave's, Jim's, Steve's, and that of ten or twelve others, none of whom did anything that directly pulled in money, as a row of numbers spinning around too fast to see, measuring the amount of cash that it took every second to bring us to work. Our salaries were based on a forty-hour week, not a thirty-five-hour week: think of the amount of money the company officially paid out every day just to finance the time all of its thousands of employees spent for lunch! In certain moods it became impossible for me to shift from my personal impression of the one small expensive subunit of the company to the overall net income figures we read every quarter on earnings reports in the internal newsletter—it was difficult to believe that money was coming in at anywhere near the rate at which we were pouring it out. And this doubtfulness would sometimes extend to companies all over the city: a skyline's worth of overreaching expenditure, a whole corporate stratum existing at an unsustainably high standard—the white paper towel standard, rather than the hot air blower standard.

When I would say to Dave or Sue that I sometimes wondered how we, or any company, could afford its operating expenses, they would smile at me charitably and say, "Don't worry, we can afford it, *believe* me." But they knew no better than I did. Just because it is convention to have one thousand business cards printed up for you the week after you are hired, even though, unless you are a salesman or you do a lot of recruiting, you will probably give out no more than thirty in the course of your whole employment, most of them in the first year to relatives, and later only on occasions in which the giving out of the business card adds a coy irony to some interchange, and even though the possession of business cards has no other function, really, than to demonstrate good faith on the company's part, to make you feel that you belong there right from the beginning, no matter how valueless you may seem to yourself to be in the first three months—just because this level of luxury is conventional, and the price schedules at printers' encourage volume, doesn't mean that it and things like it might not at some point pull the whole structure of wasteful, half-understood, inherited convention right down.[1] We came in to work every day and were treated like popes—a new manila folder for every task; expensive courier services; taxi vouchers; trips to three-day fifteen-hundred-dollar conferences to keep us up to date in our fields; even the dinkiest chart or memo typed, xeroxed, distributed, and filed; overhead transparencies to elevate the most casual meeting into something important and official; every trash can in the whole corporation, over ten thousand trash cans, emptied and fitted with a fresh bag every night; restrooms with at least one more sink than ever conceivably would be in use at any one time,

[1] When you leave a job, one of the hardest decisions you have to make on cleaning out your desk is what to do with the coffinlike cardboard tray holding 958 fresh-smelling business cards. You can't throw them out—they and the nameplate and a few sample payroll stubs are proof to yourself that you once showed up at that building every day and solved complicated, utterly absorbing problems there; unfortunately, the problems themselves, though they once obsessed you, and kept you working late night after night, and made you talk in your sleep, turn out to have been hollow: two weeks after your last day they already have contracted into inert pellets one-fiftieth their former size; you find yourself unable to recreate the sense of what was really at stake, for it seems to have been the Hungarian 5/2 rhythm of the lived workweek alone that kept each fascinating crisis inflated to its full interdepartmental complexity. But coterminously, while the problems you were paid to solve collapse, the nod of the security guard, his sign-in book, the escalator ride, the things on your desk, the sight of colleagues' offices, their faces seen from characteristic angles, the features of the corporate bathroom, all miraculously expand: and in this way what was central and what was incidental end up exactly reversed.

ornamented with slabs of marble that would have done credit to the restrooms of the Vatican! What were we participating in here?[1]

But despite this sort of periodic metascruple, I certainly helped myself to the paper towels. Now I briskly pulled five of them from the diamond-shaped opening: one to wash my face with, two to rinse it, a fourth to dry it, and a fifth to dry my glasses when I had rinsed them. Each time I pulled, a new but identical towel-flap was there for me to grasp: if you had blinked at the right moment, you might never have known that it was different from the towel you had been looking at; but it was! This renewing of newness—whether it was

- the appearance of another identical Pez tablet at the neck of the plastic Pez elevator, or
- the sight of one parachutist after another standing for a second in the door of an airplane before he jumped, or
- the rolling-into-position of a pinball after the previous one had escaped your flippers, or
- one sticky disk of sliced banana displaced from its spot on the knife over the cereal bowl by its successor, or
- the uprising of yet another step of the escalator,

was for me then, and is still, one of the greatest sources of happiness that the man-made world can offer. And it remains a matter of some personal frustration to me that fast-food restaurants, which offer so much of this kind of patterned mechanical renewal (as in the spring-loaded holes from which one Styrofoam cup after another emerges), consistently interfere with the pleasure we might take in it by (a) failing to stress

[1] And from this wealth and pomp we return home every evening and stand sweating in front of a chest of drawers, some hanging open, no ball bearings at all, and put the briefcase and the bag from the convenience store down on the floor and begin to pull handfuls of change and stubs of Velamints packs out of our pockets, forced to lean forward slightly in order to cup all the unwanted coinage we have collected from the world that day because we have lazily used whole bills for every transaction, dropping the warm change and keys and cash-machine receipts and litter into a saucer that is already overflowing with change, and then assuming another special *contrapposto* pose to pull out the wallet, whose moist bulk was a subliminal bother all day, although we weren't able to pinpoint our discomfort until now, as we drop the slightly sticky lump of leather and plastic on top of the sliding mound of change and feel one whole cheek of our ass instantly cool down, relieved of ten hours of this remorid propinquity. And we store our pants away, ensuring that the

to their employees the extreme importance of loading the black-and-chrome table-napkin dispensers with the napkins pointing in the right direction: not backward, with flap-folds hidden, so that to get two napkins out you have to pinch a bulge of six or more at a time and wrestle them all through the chrome mouth at once, leaving the guilty excess on top, where nobody will use them because nobody will trust them; or if they don't do that by (b) allowing their people to stuff the dispenser full far beyond its capacity, carried away by the admittedly impressive number of napkins it can hold, so that the flap you pull tears or draws the machine shuddering on its rubber nubs over the countertop—frustrating because here is an invention that is simple, long-lived, life-enhancing, ingenious, and that could easily be one of those pings of small-time pleasure in your fast-food meal, and yet through ignorance or carelessness its greatness is consistently traduced, and as a result millions of table napkins are thrown away without having served their purpose. But I am confident that the food chains will recognize this common mistake in time and institute training procedures that have their new-hires chanting, "Flaps to the front! Flaps to the front!"; and they will trade in all of those hot-air blowers for the hazards of towel waste—just as the floating straw has been, at least by some vendors, recently made heavy enough to stay put in a carbonated environment.[1]

---

creases are reinstated for later wearings by holding the pants upside down by their cuffs and bringing them up through the triangle of the clotheshanger with its specially treated no-slip cardboard tube and letting them fall in half over it, knowing that though the pants are a bit sweaty now, they will be all fresh-seeming by day after tomorrow when we will need to wear them again. We walk around in our underpants and T-shirt waiting for the Ronzoni shells to boil. Can this disorganized, do-it-yourself evening life really be the same life as the clean, noble, Pendaflex life we lead in office buildings?

[1] Let me mention another fairly important development in the history of the straw. I recently noticed, and remembered dimly half noticing for several years before then, that the paper wrapper, which once had slipped so easily down the plastic straw and bunched itself into a compressed concertina which you could use to perform traditional bar and dorm tricks with, now does not slip at all. It hugs the straw's surface so closely that even though the straw itself is stiffer than the earlier paper straw, the plastic sometimes buckles under the force you end up using in trying to push the wrapper down the old habitual way. A whole evolved method for unwrapping

I opened the first of the five towels under the hot water, folded it in half wet, and tapped just a half-squirt of pink soap onto it, which I diluted with another quick pass under the tap. Then, bending low over the sink, my tie clamped out of harm's way under one elbow, I raised the dripping folio in both hands and blinded myself in its warmth. I scrubbed. The wings of my nose were held closed by the sides of my little fingers. I said, "Oh God" into the sopping paper, immeasurably soothed. Face-washing seems to work as acupuncture is said to: the sudden signals of warmth flooding your brain from the nerves of the face, especially the eyelids, unmoor your thinking for an instant, dislodging your attention from any thoughts that had been in progress and causing it to slide back randomly to the first fixed spot in memory that it finds—often a subject that you had left unresolved earlier in the day which returns now as an image magnified against the grainy blackness of your closed eyelids.

---

straws—one-handed, very like rapping a cigarette on a table to ensure that the tobacco was firmly settled into the tube—now no longer works, and we must pinch off the tip of the wrapper and tear our way two-handedly all the way down the seam as if we were opening a piece of junk mail. But I have faith that this mistake too will be corrected; and we may someday even be nostalgic about the period of several years when straws were difficult to unwrap. It is impossible to foresee the things that go wrong in these small innovations, and it takes time for them to be understood as evils and acted upon. Similarly, there are often unexpected plusses to some minor new development. What sugar-packet manufacturer could have known that people would take to flapping the packet back and forth to centrifuge its contents to the bottom, so that they could handily tear off the top? The nakedness of a simple novelty in pre-portioned packaging has been surrounded and softened and made sense of by gesticulative adaptation (possibly inspired by the extinguishing oscillation of a match after the lighting of a cigarette); convenience has given rise to ballet; and the sound of those flapping sugar packets in the early morning, fluttering over from nearby booths, is not one I would willingly forgo, even though I take my coffee unsweetened. Nobody could have predicted that maintenance men would polish escalator handrails standing still, or that students would discover that you can flip pats of pre-portioned butter so they stick to the wall, or that tradesmen would discover that they could conveniently store pencils behind their ears, or later that they would gradually *stop* storing pencils behind their ears, or that windshield wipers could serve as handy places to leave advertising flyers. An unpretentious technical invention—the straw, the sugar packet, the pencil, the windshield wiper—has been ornamented by a mute folklore of behavioral inventions, unregistered, unpatented, adopted and fine-tuned without comment or thought.

In my case, the image that returned was the broken shoelace as it had appeared just before I had repaired it in my office seven minutes before. The question then had been, how come my shoelaces broke within some twenty-eight hours of each other, after two years of continuous use? Now I relived the first sensations of pulling the lace-ends up tight before I had begun the knot: it was a pull that seemed to involve about an inch of lace friction. I compared it with the important second pull, often a much harder pull, a real yank, or even two, I did to tighten the twist of the overhand base knot. You yanked in a floorward direction in this second pull, and the friction seemed to be confined to about a quarter of an inch of lace length—so *that,* I now thought, was where the real concentrated wear would have occurred. I felt I was making progress. As I rinsed my face with the second and third paper towels, I tried again to incorporate in my explanation of the dual breakage the additional contribution of walking flexion to total shoelace wear, since the stresses of walking, while individually small, were repeated thousands of times—for example, even in walking just now from my office to the men's room, I must have flexed each shoe and therefore exerted tension and friction on its lace thirty or forty times. I turned off the water and began absent-mindedly drying my face with the fourth towel.

What I needed was a way to discriminate between the kind of wear inflicted by pulling on the laces with my hands and the kind that came about as I walked. And this time, I came up with what looked to be a simple either/or test. Since my feet are mirror images of each other, and since I have no limp, the fraying under a purely walking-flex model of wear would be greatest at either both *inside* or both *outside* top eyelets—never at, say, the left shoe's inside eyelet and the right shoe's outside eyelet. My arms, on the other hand, perform their tying pulls asymmetrically, not only because my right arm is stronger than my left, as we know from murder mysteries, but also because I hold the left and right lace-ends in a subtly different grip, in readiness for the movements I will be making in forming the two bunny's ears. This allows us to determine very easily whether the chronic walk-flex or acute pull-fray model is dominant. Assume, I said to myself, that the shoelace on my right shoe that had snapped yesterday morning in my apartment had snapped at the left, or inside, top eyelet. Under walk-flex I would predict that the shoelace found in the right, or inside, top eyelet of my left shoe would have snapped today, maintaining symmetry. Conversely, under pull-fray, I would expect the left eyelet of the left shoe to have been the point of breakage. I couldn't remember, though, which two eyelets had really been involved.

I rinsed my glasses quickly under the tap, eager to be able to study my shoes in detail once again; I polished the lenses with the fifth paper towel, making bribe-me, bribe-me finger motions over the two curved surfaces until they were dry. A toilet began roaring. I stepped back from the sink and brought my glasses toward my face, enjoying the approach of those two reservoirs of widening distinctness; as I hooked the side-pieces over my ears, I raised my eyebrows, for unknown reasons.[1] Now I could see my shoes.

What I saw was a left shoe displaying a broken and repaired stretch of shoelace at the left top eyelet, and a right shoe *also* displaying a broken and repaired stretch of shoelace at its left top eyelet. This was not symmetrical, and consequently pull-fray was dominant and walk-flex discountable as a source of wear. Good. But: these test results forced me to reconsider the whole earlier problem of how to make sense of the large percentage of random daytime comings-undone and retyings. And there I abandoned the topic, because Abelardo, my manager, emerged from a stall.

"What do you think, Howie?" he said; it was his standard greeting—one I was fond of.

"Abe, I don't know what to think," I said; my standard response. I adjusted my glasses in the mirror so that they weren't crooked, knowing that they would revert to their normal slight skew in five minutes.

"Lunchtime?" said Abe, scrubbing his hands.

[1] People seem to raise their eyebrows whenever they bring something close to their faces. The first sip of a morning cup of coffee makes you raise your eyebrows; I have seen some individuals displace their entire scalp along with their eyebrows whenever they bring a forkful of food to their mouths. A possible explanation is that eyebrow-raising is a way of telling your brain not to activate the natural flinch reaction that the approach of moving objects near the face normally triggers.

"Yep. Got to buy shoelaces. One popped yesterday, the other popped today."

"Well well."

"It mystifies me. Has that ever happened to you?"

"No. I use a fresh pair every day."

"Oh? You buy them at CVS, or where?"

"I have them flown in. UPS blue. An Indian guy in Texas makes them for me. He blends alpaca and some of the finer tweeds. Then he sprays it with Krylon."

"Nice," I said. The secret to working for Abe was realizing that nothing he said, outside of company business, was serious or true. "Take it easy."

"Yep."

Approaching the door, I began to whistle loudly. I pulled on the handle; the door swung toward me fast with no resistance.

"Oop," I said.

"Oop," said Ron Nemick, entering.

I held the door for him. As I walked out into the hall, I realized that the tune I had just begun was "I'm a Yankee Doodle Dandy."

From within, I heard Abe cheerfully start up with "I Knew an Old Lady Who Swallowed a Fly."

Chapter Twelve

LESS THAN AN HOUR later, I stood in the pose of George Washington crossing the Potomac, one foot on a higher step, one hand on the handrail, gliding steadily upward on the diagonal between the lobby and my destination. The sound of the escalator's motor had become indistinct, although I could still feel a faint rhythm of clicks transmitted through the steps, which I assumed were caused as the links of the chain that drew me upward were engaged by the sprockets at either end; and the sounds of the lobby, too, were blurred and assimilated into a universal lobby-sound, as if each unitary tock of a secretary's heel were a sharp brush-point of pigment touched to a wash-covered watercolor, flaring palely outward. From this height, the height of sociology and statistics, foreshortened employees moved in visible patterns: they were propelled one by one at a fixed speed into the lobby by the revolving door; they coalesced in front of elevators whose arrival dinger had just lit; they renewed the permanent four-person line at the cash machine; occasionally two of them, on intersecting rushed trajectories, would raise their arms in joyful surprise and exchange civilities while sidestepping in a neat clockwise semicircle in order to continue backward on their way, each held for an obligatory moment in the other's gravitational field and then, by mutual consent, completing their loop-the-loop by turning and hurrying on.

I had not moved my hand from its first grip on the handrail, but because the handrail progressed upward on its track at an imperceptibly slower speed than the steps did (slippage?), my arm was in a different position, my elbow more bent, than when I had begun. I repositioned my hand ahead of me. It was strange to think that because of the difference in speeds, these escalator steps must periodically lap the handrail that accompanied them: since the slippage on my escalator was about a foot per up trip, or two feet per complete cycle, over an estimated complete handrail loop of a hundred feet, the handrail was lapped by the moving stairway every fifty revolutions—like those stock cars with fewer decals that you think are running neck and neck with Foyt or Unser, but are in fact laps and laps off the pace, driven by what kind of men? Sad, disappointed men, you instinctively feel; but maybe novices or fanatics, delighted to be there at all.

That the handrail didn't progress at exactly the same speed as the steps was an observation I owed to my lately acquired habit of standing still and gliding for the entire ride, rather than walking up the steps. I had switched to gliding only after I had been working at the company for about a year. Before taking the job, I had used escalators relatively infrequently, at airports, malls, certain subway exits, and department stores, and on these occasions I had gradually developed strong beliefs as to the proper way to ride them. Your role was to advance at the normal rate you climbed stairs at home, allowing the motor to supplement, *not replace,* your own physical efforts. Otis, Montgomery, and Westinghouse had not meant for you to falter after a step or two on their machines and finally halt, arriving at the top later than you would had you briskly mounted a fixed, unelectrified flight. They would never have devoted fortunes of development money and man-years of mechanical ingenuity in order to construct a machine possessing all the external characteristics of a regular set of stairs, including individual steps, a practicable grade, and a shiny banister, just so that healthy people like me could stand in states of suspended animation, our eyes in test patterns of vacancy, until we were deposited on the upper level. Their inspiration had not been the chair lift or the cog railway, but the moped, which you helped out with leg power on hills. *Yet people refused to see this.* Often in department stores I would get stuck behind two motionless passengers and want to seize their shoulders and urge them on, like an instructor at an Outward Bound program, saying, "Annette, Bruce—this isn't the Land of the Lotus-Eaters. You're on a moving stairway. *Feel* your own effortful, bobbing steps melt into the inexhaustible meliorism of the escalator. Watch the angles of floors and escalator ceilings above and around you alter their vanishing points at a syrupy speed that doesn't correlate with what your legs are telling you they are doing. Don't you see that when you two stop, two abreast, you are not only blocking me? Don't you see that you indicate to all those who are right now stepping onto the escalator at the bottom and looking timidly up for inspiration that if they bound eagerly up they too will catch up with us and be thwarted in their advance? They were wavering whether to stand or to climb, and you just sapped their wills! *You made them choose to waste their time!* And they in turn impede those who follow them—thus you perpetuate a pattern of sloth and congestion that may persist for hours. *Can't you see that*?" Sometimes I rudely halted at the step just below the one the pair stood on, my face a caricature of pointless impatience, tailgating them until (often with startled sounds and offered apologies I didn't deserve) they doubled up to let me pass. Headway was easier to establish going down, because the rapid thump of my steps would scare them over to one side.

But a year of riding the escalator to work changed me. Now I was a passenger on the machine four times a day—sometimes six or more, if I had to redescend to the lobby to take the elevator to one of the company's departments on the twenty-sixth or -seventh floor—and the habitual thoughts that the experience had previously called forth became too familiar at that frequency. My total appreciation for the escalator deepened, eventually becoming embedded along my spinal column, but each individual ride was no longer guaranteed to trigger a well-worn piece of theory or state of irritation. I began to care less whether the original intent of the invention had been to emulate the stairway or not. And when I went back to department stores after those early months of work, I regarded the big motionless backs of shoppers ahead of me on the crowded slope with new interest, and I relaxed with them: it was natural, it was understandable, it was defensible to want to stand like an Easter Island monument in this trance of motorized ascension through architectures of retailing. Fairly early on, riding up to Housewares to buy a Revere saucepan to pair with my Teflon fry pan and complete my kitchen,[1] I even put my shopping bag (which contained a suit, a shirt, a tie, and, in a separate smaller bag from Radio Shack, a longer telephone cord) down on the step beside me and closed my eyes for a short while. I brought this new pleasure of standing still back with me to the workday escalations; and eventually I underwent a complete reversal: I never brought my long, leisurely trip to an early end with steps of my own, enjoying it as seasoned rail commuters enjoy the fixed interval of their train ride—and when people stumped past me I regarded them with sympathy. In special situations, the old irritation did

[1] In those first months of cooking dinner for myself, after years of eating the food that Seiler's and ARA had cooked for me, I studied with fresh interest the origination of the boiling bubbles in the Revere pan as I waited to pour in the Ronzoni shells: at the very beginning of boiling, grains of mercury broke free and rose upward only from special points on the floor of the pan, requiring a little scratch or irregularity in the metal to harbor their change of phase; later several beaded curtains of midsized spheres streamed where the parallel curves of the electric coil were most completely in contact with the pan's underside; later still, as glutinous, toad-like globes of hard boiling took over, my glasses misted—and I was reminded of being awakened by my parents years earlier from dreams in which I been trying to drink very thick shakes through impossibly slender straws. My father carried me to the bright kitchen saying cheerfully, "Croup again, croup again," his hair sticking in unusual directions, and he held me near the plume of steam coming from the small kettle that my mother had put on. I inhaled; the desire to croak melted in the branches behind my sternum, and as I breathed I thought happily about the blue gas flame pouring upward and flattening itself against the bottom of the kettle—the same flame which a few years later I was allowed to cook hot dogs over, skewering them on a dinner fork: grease from the hot dogs was released in short-lived fiery sparks, best seen if you turned off the light, though notable too for their paler yellow effects in daylight, and the heat charred to prominence the spoked pattern of the two ends of the hot dog. Anyway, once I let my glasses clear, I poured the Ronzoni shells into the tumultuous water: there was a hiss and a moment of complete, white-watered calm. Unless you stirred at that point, I found, your yield of shells would diminish, because some would stick to the bottom of the pan.

occasionally come back, especially on subway escalators; but when it did I now divided my blame between the halted pedestrians and the original designers of the machine: clearly the engineers had made the risers of the steps too tall, and the height weakened the functional correspondence between these stairs and their home counterparts, so that riders failed to feel innately that they were expected to climb.

I was now close to two-thirds of the way to the mezzanine. Behind me, at the base, the maintenance man had moved his rag to the handrail I was holding—in another revolution, my handprint would be polished away. Every few feet, my hand moved past a raised disk of burnished steel attached to the slope between the up escalator I rode and the down escalator to my left. I followed the disks with my eyes as they went by. I had never figured out what their purpose was. Did they cover the heads of large structural bolts, or were they there simply to discourage anyone who might be tempted to use the long median slope as a slide? This question, compressed into a blip of familiar curiosity, occurred to me once or twice a quarter, never urgently enough for me to remember it later and find out the answer.

Presently the metal disk that drew near was half lit by sun. Falling from dusty heights of thermal glass over a hundred-vaned, thirty-foot-long, unlooked-at, invisibly suspended lighting fixture that resembled the metal grid in an old-style ice cube tray, falling through the vacant middle reaches of lobby space, the sunlight draped itself over my escalator and continued from there, diminished by three-quarters, down into a newsstand inset into the marble at the rear of the lobby. I felt myself rise into its shape: my hand turned gold, coronas of stage-struck protein iridesced from my eyelashes; and one hinge of my glasses began to sparkle for attention. The transformation wasn't instantaneous; it seemed to take about as long as the wires in a toaster take to turn orange. It was the last good blast of lunch hour; possibly the best part of the escalator ride. My moving shadow appeared far off, sliding on the lobby floor, and then it began folding itself over the sunlit piles of magazines in the newsstand—magazines as thick as textbooks, separated by wooden dividers—*Forbes, Vogue, Playboy, Glamour, PC World, M*—so filled with ads that they made a splashing sound as you flipped through their cool, Kromekote pages. Incited by bright textures and warmth, four distinct images occurred to me in quick succession, three of them familiar, one of them new to me, each suggesting the next. I pictured:

(1) The lines of Creamsicle-colored shine on the shrink-wrapped edges of the row of record albums in my living room as they appeared in the evening when I came home from work.

(2) A discarded cigarette pack still wrapped in its cellophane; specifically, the delight of running a lawn mower over it, buzzing its glints and paper out over the dry grass.

(3) The mowed remains of a dinner roll I had seen once on a nice Saturday morning on the way to the subway. It was a potato-sized dinner roll, judging by the white shards, and bending closer, I recognized it as the kind of tasteless lovable roll that was included free with your order from a nearby Chinese takeout place. It had been mowed over where it lay that morning on the sharp slope that fell to the sidewalk (the street must have been widened at some point in the past): looking at it, I had imagined the flicker of indecision on the mower's sweaty face—"Rock?—No, a roll.—Stop?—Not on this tricky slope—Push on," and then the dip of the engine's drone and the card-shuffling spatter that followed, leaving, in place of a Chinese dinner roll, a neat circular distribution of white fragments.

(4) A giant piece of popcorn exploding in deep space. This last was a conception I had never envisioned in isolation before. Its brief appearance on the heels of the mowed roll (an image that occurred to me once every few months) was probably explained by my having bought and eaten a bag of popcorn earlier in the lunch hour.

Chapter Thirteen

I HAD NOT INTENDED to buy a bag of popcorn. Under the impetus of a big-necked man and a rushed woman behind him, the revolving door from the lobby had been circulating a little too fast; when my turn came, I took advantage of the existing momentum by milling through my slice of its pie chart without contributing any additional force, rolling up a sleeve. Outside, it was noontime, noontime! Fifteen healthy, coltish, slender trees grew out of the brick plaza a short way into the blue sky in front of my building, each casting an arrangement of potato chip–shaped shadows over its circular cast-iron trunk collar. ("Neenah Foundry Co. Neenah, Wis.") Men and women, seated on benches in the sun near raised beds of familiar corporate evergreens (cotoneaster, I think) were withdrawing wrapped delicacies from dazzling white bags. Sidewalk vendors poked in the ranked compartments of their carts, flipping metal doors back and forth. The rear of a truck with quilted metal sides was packed with sandwiches, spigots, Drake's Cakes, and cans in ice, its owner making change from the monetary calliope on his belt, filling three cups at a time without flipping on and off the coffee spigot, pointing at the next customer, all in looping, circling two-armed gestures, as I imagine master telephone operators working the old plug-

and-socket switchboards must have made—he was selling to the crew that was tearing down everything but the I beams and the front façade of a building across the street. I was hungry, but under this sunlit noon mood I needed something insubstantial and altitudinous, like a miniature can of Bluebird grapefruit juice, or half an arrowroot biscuit, or three capers rolling around a paper plate, or: popcorn. On impulse, I let a complete dollar fall into the popcorn vendress's hand and lifted a twist-tied bagful garnered from the cart's glass poppery, with its 1890s-style painted lettering and yellow heat lamps and suspended popping chamber, out of which individual white fulsomenesses were jumping from under a metal hinged flap, as if doing a circus stunt for the blank drifts that composed the audience—and I got no change back; no change at all to abrade my thigh as I walked or to overflow my bureau saucer that evening! How kind of her! As I jaywalked across several streets in the direction of the CVS, trailing the inevitable two or three particles from each handful that exceeded the mouth's capacity, moving between cars whose lacquer looked hot to the touch and pedestrians in white blouses and white pinpoint oxford shirts, I felt somewhat like an exploding popcorn myself: a dried bicuspid of American grain dropped into a lucid gold liquid pressed from less fortunate brother kernels, subjected to heat, and suddenly allowed to flourish outward in an instantaneous detonation of weightless reversal; an asteroid of Styrofoam, much larger but seemingly of less mass than before, composed of exfoliations that in bursting beyond their outer carapace were nonetheless guided into paisleys and baobabs and related white Fibonaccia by its disappearing, back-arching browned petals (which later found their way into the space between molars and gums), shapes which seemed quite Brazilian and intemperate for so North American a seed, and which seemed, despite the abrupt assumption of their final state, the convulsive, launching "pop," slowly arrived at, like risen dough or cave mushrooms.[1]

[1] You would think, after that sort of explosion, that the outcome would need time to set and firm in cooling racks, but no, you can eat the results just afterward, or you can eat them when they have waited in one of the high salted drifts warmed by the flat heating bulb with a frosted yellow blinding face and a back painted with reflective black material that has tiny scratches

It took me ten minutes to walk to the CVS pharmacy. I threw out what was left of the popcorn before I went inside, into a square can out front with a flap sticky from soft drinks: the trick here was to use whatever you were throwing out to push the flap open and then snap your hand out of the way quickly enough that the flap didn't fall back on it, a technique

---

in it through which the wattage shines. Needing an actual taste of popcorn to confirm these recollections of how it had seemed that day, I recently looked in the cupboards and found an old package of Jiffy Pop—not the new microwave Jiffy Pop, but the old aluminum Jiffy Pop, a relic of the great age of aluminum, when you tented it over turkeys, teased it off the inside of gum wrappers, froze with it, flattened out its wrinkles with your thumbnail, scraped the last crisp remnants of a Stouffer's baked spinach soufflé off its stamped and crimped sides—and more than a relic: Jiffy Pop was the finest example of the whole aluminous genre: a package inspired by the fry pan whose handle is also the hook it hangs from in the store, with a maelstrom of swirled foil on the top that, subjected to the subversion of the exploding kernels, first by the direct collisions of discrete corns and then in a general indirect uplift of the total volume of potentiated cellulose, gradually unfurls its dome, turning slowly as it despirals itself, providing in its gradual expansion a graspable, slow-motion version of what each erumpent particle of corn is undergoing invisibly and instantaneously beneath it. By the time the dome is completely deployed (I noticed, shaking it over the coils of the stove), the aluminum has revealed itself to be surprisingly thin, thinner than Reynolds Wrap—and you realize that the only reason it could withstand the first battery of direct pops was that at that point it had been strengthened by its twirls (except in the vulnerable flat center). To serve it, you tore back the thin foil in triangles, thus making bloom a flower no bee will ever fertilize: the final mannerist inflorescence, the second derivative, of the original harvested ear of corn. Besides Jiffy Pop, we had as I grew up the slightly earlier Jolly Time and TV Time—the pair of plastic tubes, one containing kernels, the other containing hydrogenated oil you squeezed out into the pan—and we were even given a popcorn popper, which was difficult to clean. But the invention of Jiffy Pop seemed to me in retrospect so much greater than any other popcorn-related product, including all microwavables, seemed in fact one of the outstanding instances of human ingenuity in my lifetime, that after I had eaten a few handfuls, I went to a university library and found out the name of the inventor, Frederick Mennen, made copies of the relevant patents (". . . a wrinkled foil cover sheet adapted to be extended by expansion of container contents generated by cooking . . ."), and found a 1960 picture of him, smiling sad-eyedly in his factory in La Porte, Indiana, while behind him women in lab coats kept an eye on the conveyor belt. The first patent appeared in the *U.S. Patent Gazette* in 1957, a few months after I was born. I got Mennen's home number from information and called him to congratulate him, thirty years after the fact, and to ask him whether he was prouder of the spiral package itself, or of the elegant machine he had invented to impart the spiral to the package. The phone rang six times; growing shyer with each ring, and worrying that he might have died, I hung up, dreading a widow's frail answer.

that didn't work perfectly in this case because the receptacle was overfull and I had to crush my popcorn bag down into earlier trash so that the flap could swing shut properly. I wiped popcorn salt and oil from my hands onto the inside of my pants pockets and entered the coolness of the store.

I had no idea where the shoelaces were kept, but I was a frequent customer of CVSes all over the city, and considered myself an old hand at their layouts and their odd systems of classification. "eye care," "headache," "hair notions," read the suspended placards, with a once catchy, now dated absence of initial capitals—but few, I thought, knew as I did to find earplugs in a far aisle called "first aid," near swimmer's nose-clips, Ace knee supporters, Cruex, Caladryl, Li-Ban lice-killing spray, and the Band-Aid shelves. In fact, most of my familiarity with CVS stores had come from my regular purchase of earplugs. I used a box or more of them a week, and over the years I had grown fond of their recherché placement, implying, which was often true, that hearing was an affliction, a symptom to be cured. The aisle, moreover, was never crowded with pill-studiers, as "headache" was, and all of those nearby boxes of Band-Aids, still trustingly unsealed, with specialized shapes for unusual wounds and the bonus row of miniature strips that adults used even for quite bad finger-cuts, such as you get slicing through a presliced bagel, because they were less ostentatious and self-pitying than the standard size, seemed to me to be the heart of the whole pharmacy. Incidentally, if you open a Band-Aid box, it will exhale a smell (as I found out recently, needing a Band-Aid for a surprisingly gruesome little cut[1]) that will shoot you directly back to when you were four[2]—although I don't trust this

[1] I borrowed the Band-Aid from the box in L.'s apartment—I did not own a box of Band-Aids myself. And very often you see women wistfully studying the Band-Aid shelves at CVS: perhaps they are thinking, If I buy these Band-Aids, I will have them to put in my medicine cabinet, ready to dress the minor wounds of the good man I will maybe meet at some future date, and later they will be there for the elbow scrapes of the children I will have with him.

[2] At that age I once stabbed my best friend, Fred, with a pair of pinking shears in the base of the neck, enraged because he had been given the comprehensive sixty-four-crayon Crayola box—including the gold and silver crayons—and would not let me look closely at the box to see how Crayola had stabilized the built-in crayon sharpener under the tiers of crayons. Over the next week and a half, Fred, very aloof, worked his way

olfactory memory trick anymore, because it seems to be a hardware bug in the neural workings of the sense of smell, a low-level sort of tie-in, underneath subtler strata of language and experience, between smell, vision, and self-love, which has been mistakenly exalted by some writers as something realer and purer and more sacredly significant than intellective memory, like the bubbles of swamp methane that awed provincials once took for UFOs.

I used a lot of earplugs, not only to get to sleep, but also at work, because I had found that the magnified Sensurround sounds of my own jaw and teeth, and the feeling of underwater fullness in my ears, and the muffling of all external noise, even the printing of my own calculator or the sliding of one piece of paper over another, helped me to concentrate. On some days, writing impassioned memos to senior management, I spent the whole morning and afternoon wearing earplugs—wearing them even to the men's room, and taking only one out to talk on the phone. Lunch hours I never wore them; and possibly this explained why my thoughts had a different kind of upper harmonic during lunch: it wasn't just the sunlight and the clean glasses, it was also that I heard the world distinctly for the first time since walking to the subway in the morning. (I wore them in the subway, too.) I used Flents Silaflex silicone earplugs. Only since 1982 or so have these superb plugs been generally available, at least in the stores I visit. Before that I used the old Flents stopples, in the orange box—they were made of cotton impregnated with wax, and they were huge: you had to cut them in half with a pair of scissors to get a shape that would stay put when you worked it in place, and they left your fingers greasy with pink paraffin. They revolted L., who used to store any I left on her bedside windowsill in an empty pastilles canister with a rural scene on it—and I don't blame her. Then a company called McKeon

---

through every size and style of Band-Aid that Johnson & Johnson made (his family, rich, could afford the comprehensive variety box, which included shapes that no longer exist, to my knowledge), refusing to show me the (very minor) wound, stringing out my guilt and curiosity by wearing the smallest Band-Aid, a tiny flesh-colored fried egg three-eighths of an inch across, long after I was sure he had only a faint white asterisk of a scar underneath.

Products began to be a force in the market, offering Mack's Pillow Soft® earplugs—lumps of transparent gel-like putty that made a seal so complete that your eardrums ached slightly as you released the pressure from your fingers, because they were creating a mild vacuum in your ear canal—a vacuum! We all know how poorly sound travels in a vacuum! These new plugs, then, were not merely blocking soundwaves from passing through, they were altering the sonic characteristics of the very air resident in the canal! Their fame spread from drug chain to drug chain by word of mouth. I wore them until I forgot what true sound was. Flents counteracted powerfully, pushing their sleek Silaflex model—flesh-colored cylindrical versions of Mack's—while gradually phasing out the old wax-and-cotton Tootsie Roll behemoths. The Silaflex plugs, like Mack's, were sold in a plastic snap-open carrying case, like a snuffbox; I carried the case around in my shirt pocket so that I could have new earplugs whenever I needed them. Fearing lawsuits, perhaps, Flents continued to oversize the newer product—though the package said "3 pairs in handy storage box," I still twisted each cylinder in half and got six complete sets. In bed I kissed L. good night while she wrote down the events of her day in a spiral notebook, and then I selected a promising used plug from the array on my bedside table and pressed it into whichever ear was going to point toward the ceiling first. If she asked a question after I had put the plug in and turned on my side, I had to raise my head off the pillow, exposing the lower ear, to hear her. Earlier I had tried sleeping with earplugs in both ears, so that I would be sound-free as I revolved in my sleep, no matter which ear turned up, but what I found was that the pillow ear would be in pain by the early hours of the morning; so I learned how to transfer the single warm plug from ear to ear in my sleep whenever I turned. By this time L. was resigned to my wearing them; sometimes, to demonstrate special tenderness, she would get the wooden toaster tongs, take hold of an earplug with them, drop it in my ceilingward ear before I had gotten around to doing so, and tamp it in place, saying, "You see? You see how much I love you?"[1]

[1] Although earplugs are essential for getting to sleep, they are useless later on, when you are awakened with night anxieties, and your brain is steeping in a bad fluorescent juice. I slept beautifully through college, but the new job

Just over from earplugs were the long-nosed white bottles of ear-wax dissolver, which I bought once a year or so. Whenever you discovered, on removing the night's earplug after your alarm went off, that you did not hear any better with it out, you remained in bed and squirted the cold carbamide peroxide solution into your ear and lay motionless, waiting for a tactile ferment of bubbling to begin. Then you took a shower. It is true that this squirt of reagent wasn't as effective as the mind-boggling steel warm-water blaster that nurses used: that device had two syringal finger-hooks and a thumb-actuated plunger, and it sent an almost unendurable surge of warm water into your head, flushing impurities out into a bedpan you held steady at your neck. After I had had my ears roared clean that way, I heard reaches of the hertzian range that I had not heard probably since I was newborn; and the greatest

---

brought regular insomnia, and with it a long period of trial and error, until I hit on the images that most consistently lured me back to sleep. I began with Monday Night at the Movies title sequences: a noun like "MEMORANDUM" or "CALAMARI" in huge three-dimensional curving letters, outlined with chrome edgework of lines and blinking stars, rotating on two axes. I meant myself to be asleep by the time I passed through the expanding O, or the dormer window of the A. This did not work for long. In the belief that images with more substance to them, and less abstract pattern, would encourage the dreaming state, I pictured myself driving in a low fast car, taking off from an aircraft carrier in a low fast plane, or twisting water from a towel in a flooded basement. The plane worked best, but it didn't work well. And then, surprised that I had taken so long to think of it, I remembered the convention of counting sheep. In Disney cartoons a little scene of sheep springing lightly over a stile or a picket fence appears in a thought-cloud above the man in the bed, while on the soundtrack violins accompany a soft voice out of 78 records saying, "One, two, three, four . . ." I thought of story conferences in Disney studios back in the golden days of cartoons: the look of benign concentration on the crouching animator's face as he carefully colored in the outline of a suspended stylized sheep one frame farther along in its arc, warm light from his clamp-on drafting-table lamp shining over the pushpins and masking tape and the special acetate pencil in his hand—I was soon successfully asleep. But though this Disney version achieved its purpose, it felt unsatisfactory: I was imagining sheep, true, but the convention, which I wanted to uphold, called for *counting* them. Yet I didn't feel that there was any point to counting what was obviously the same set of animated frames recycled over and over. I needed to pierce through the cartoon, and create a procession of truly differentiable sheep for myself. So I homed in on each one in its approach to the hurdle and looked for individuating features—some thistle prominently caught, or a bit of dried mud on a shank. Some times I strapped a number on the next one to jump and gave him a Kentucky Derby name: Brunch Commander, Nosferatu, I Before E, Wee Willie

pleasure in hearing this new wheat-field crispness overlaid on normal sound was in being able to bottle it away when I wanted to with a pair of Silaflex earplugs. But I was embarrassed to ask a nurse to use the ear-blaster on me because she would see the impurities gush from my ear, so I often resorted to the do-it-yourself white bottle of CVS solvent, and afterward stood in the shower for the count of sixty with my head at an angle that allowed the hot water to enter my ear with as

---

Winkie. And I made him take the jump very slowly, so that I could study every phase of it—the crumbs of airborne dirt floating slowly toward the lens, the soft-lipped grimace, the ripple moving through the wool on landing. If I wasn't off by then, I backed up and reconstructed the sheep's entire day; for I found that it was the *approach* to the jump, rather than the jump itself, that was sleep-inducing. Some sheep had probably reported for work around noon several towns over, tousled and fractious. Around two in the afternoon, while at my office, expecting a rough night, I had (I imagined) placed a call to one of the shepherd-dispatchers: Could she send out some random number of sheep not larger than thirty to arrive outside my apartment by 3:30 A.M., for counting? The practiced crook of the sheep dispatcher travels over her herd, pointing: "You, you, you"; she repeats my address again and again to her nodding subjects; and my personal flock departs fifteen minutes later, with a voucher to be signed on arrival. All that afternoon they cross village greens, wade brooks, and trot along the median valleys of highways. While I am eating dinner with L., they are still miles away, but by bedtime, 11:30 P.M., I can spot them with my binoculars coming over a rise: tiny bobbing shapes next to a foreshortened Red Roof Inn sign, still in the next county. And at 3:30 A.M., when I need them badly, they bustle up, exhilarated from their journey: I put aside the unwritten thank-you letter I have been writhing over, log the sheep in and pay them off, and the first few begin lofting themselves over the planks and milk crates I have assembled out front, their small pink tongues visible with the effort, the whites of their sheep eyes showing; one, two, three . . . and then I have become a very successful director of fabric-softener commercials—the agency needs lush shots of jumping sheep; their fleece has to read as golden in the failing sunlight, and the greens of the countryside have to be inconceivably full-throated. I shampoo each sheep myself; I comfort the weepers; I read to the assembled flock from Cardinal Newman's *Idea of a University* to heighten their sense of purpose and grace, and I demonstrate to them how I need them to *send* their plump torsos airborne, hike *up* their rear legs for an added boost, *throw* their heads back for drama, and always, always lead in their landing with the left forehoof. I give them their cue through a rolled-up script: "Okay, number four. Lighter footfalls. Now thrust. Up. And the rear legs! More teeth! Show strain! Now some nostril! And over!" Lately I have found that the last thing in my mind before resumed unconsciousness is often the dwindling sight of one lone sheep, who, having cleared my hurdle and been checked off, full of relief and the glow of accomplishment, is hurrying over farther hills to his next assignment, which is to leap an herbal border in slow motion for L., awake with worries of her own beside me.

much flushing directness as possible. This was the kind of important and secretive product that CVS stores sold—they were a whole chain dedicated to making available the small, expensive, highly specialized items that readied human bodies for human civilization. Men and women eyed each other strangely here—unusual forces of attraction and furtiveness were at work. Things were for sale whose use demanded nudity and privacy. It was more a woman's store than a man's store, but men were allowed to roam with complete freedom past shelves that glowed with low but measurable curie-levels of luridness. You slip by a woman reading the fine print on a disposable vinegar douche kit. She feels you pass. *Frisson!* Another woman is contemplating a box of Aspercreme—what for? A third is deciding whether she wants a Revlon eyelash curler, which looks like a cross between a tea strainer and a medieval catapult. Heavy curved soaps like Basis and Dove, though sold in perky square boxes, will be slid from their packaging for tonight's shower: their cream-molded trademarks will be worn away by their passage over womanly upper arms and stomachs.[1] When I was younger than I should have been, I used to steal sanitary napkins from the box among the shoes in my parents' closet, where they lay folded like tennis sweaters in a drawer, and take them to the bathroom with me, where I would with some difficulty poke a hole in one of them, using a pencil or a toothbrush, push my crayon-sized penis through the hole, and urinate into the toilet—and CVS stores have some of this uncertain, childish kinkiness and indirection to them, mixing so many kinds of privateness together in one public store. Even if you are there just to buy some decongestant or, as I was, simply for a pair of shoelaces, you feel the subdued tantalization of the place: the Coppertone billboards used as wallpaper, square yards of tanned shoulders and knees and faces; Krazy Nails wallpaper, too; and Maalox and Secret antiperspirant and Energizer battery wallpaper, all of the ex-billboards cropped and overlapping, obscured here and there by circular antitheft mirrors. Deeply confidential names whispered up at you from every

[1] There is no good word for *stomach;* just as there is no good word for *girlfriend. Stomach* is to *girlfriend* as *belly* is to *lover,* and as *abdomen* is to *consort,* and as *middle* is to *petite amie.*

aisle—Anbesol, Pamprin, Evenflo, Tronolane—masterly syllabic splicings of the perverted and the doctorly, the pattern of each color package repeated in piles of four and eight and ten on the shelf. It was a whole Istanbul of the medicine cabinet, insulated from the street by the Red Cross innocence and purity of the CVS sign.

And here were the shampoos! Was there really any need to study the historical past of Chandragupta of Pataliputra, or Harsha of Kanauj, the rise of the Chola kings of Tanjore and the fall of the Pallava kings of Kanchi, who once built the Seven Pagodas of Mahabalipuram, or the final desolation and ruin of the great metropolis of Vijayanagar, when we had dynastic shifts, turbulence, and plenty of lather in the last twenty years of that great Hindu inheritance, shampoo? Yes, there was. Yet emotional analogies were not hard to find between the history of civilization on the one hand and the history within the CVS pharmacy on the other, when you caught sight of a once great shampoo like Alberto VO5 or Prell now in sorry vassalage on the bottom shelf of aisle 1B, overrun by later waves of Mongols, Muslims, and Chalukyas—Suave; Clairol Herbal Essence; Gee, Your Hair Smells Terrific; Silkience; Finesse; and bottle after bottle of the Akbaresque Flex. Prell's green is too simple a green for us now; the false French of its name seems kitschy, not chic, and where once it was enveloped in my TV-soaked mind by the immediacy and throatiness of womanly voice-overs, it is now late in its decline, lightly advertised, having descended year by year through the thick but hygroscopic emulsions of our esteem, like the large descending pearl that was used in one of its greatest early ads to prove how lusciously rich it was. (I *think* that ad was for Prell—or was it Breck, or Alberto VO5?[1]) I remember friends' older sisters who used those old sham-

[1] And was it Prell concentrate or Head & Shoulders where the new unbreakable tube squirted from the showerer's fingers ("Oops!") over the glass shower stall, caught by the husband who studied it with wonderment? *Manageability*—the romance of the notion would come back if I paused in the shampoo aisle for a minute: so Harold Geneenian a word to be murmured by models whose hair looked like Samantha's on *Bewitched.* And I would recall the family who, more in sorrow than in anger, told their father please not to wear his blue blazer because of dandruff flaking, until after he used Head & Shoulders (a repulsive name for a shampoo, when you think of

poos—one sister especially, fresh from using Alberto VO5 and Dippity-do, with her hair rolled up in a number of small pink foam curlers and three RC cola cans, sitting down at the kitchen table to eat breakfast while we (nine years old) ate raw Bermuda onions for lunch, reading Fester Bestertester paperbacks. I think of the old product managers staring out the window like Proust, reminiscing about the great days when they had huge TV budgets and everything was hopping, now reduced to leafing through trade magazines to keep up with late-breaking news in hair care like outsiders. *Soon, nobody would know that they had introduced a better kind of plastic for their shampoo bottle, a kind with a slight matte gunmetal dullness to it instead of the unpleasant patent-leathery reflectivity of then existing efforts at transparency; that with it they had taken their product straight to the top!* In time, once everyone had died who had used a certain discontinued brand of shampoo, so that it passed from living memory, it no longer would be understood properly, correctly situated in the felt periphery of life; instead it would be one of many quaint vials of plastic in country antique stores—understood no better than a ninth-century trinket unearthed on the Coromandel coast. I am not proud of the fact that major ingredients of my emotional history are available for purchase today at CVS. The fact seems especially puzzling, since mine was entirely a spectator's emotion: I did not use any of the great shampoos; instead I exhausted innumerable bars of Ivory soap on my hair (the bars turned concave as they diminished, fitting my skull), at least until a year into my job on the mezzanine, when hair began to leave my head and I, trying to undo the years of soapy harshness that I thought might have been the cause of the departure, switched to Johnson's baby shampoo.

Eventually, as products continue to be launched year after year, your original shampoo pantheon, or toothpaste or vending machine or magazine or car or felt-tip pen pantheon, becomes infiltrated by novelty, and you may find yourself losing your points of reference, unable to place a new item in a

---

it, but you never do); and the woman whose life was so busy that she used an aerosol shampoo-in-a-can in the privacy of the elevator, brushing her oiliness away, exiting twenty floors up with glossy highlights.

comparative nest of familiar brand names because the other names still themselves feel raw and unassimilated. In shampoos, I think I have reached that point; the Flex family wore me down finally and I am now living exclusively in the past: short of something really spectacular, any post-Flex product (like this Swedish birch-and-chamomile stuff, Hälsa) will remain dead for me, external to my life, no matter how many times I see it on the shelf. Theoretically, I suppose there is a point, too, at which the combined volume of all the miniature histories of miscellanea that have been collecting in parallel in my memory, covering a number of the different aisles of CVS and even some of the handiwork of civilization at large, will reach some critical point and leave me saturated, listless, unable to entertain a single new enthusiasm; I expect it to happen when the CVS stores themselves have become sad and dated, like Rite Aids or Oscos before them: the red letters and stapled white bags bowing before something we can't even imagine, something even cleaner, electrifyingly chipper.[1]

For now, though, the CVS pharmacy is closer to the center of life than, say, Crate & Barrel or Pier 1, or restaurants, national parks, airports, research triangles, the lobbies of office buildings, or banks. Those places are the novels of the period, while CVS is its diary. And somewhere within this particular store, according to Tina, who knew it much better than I did, was a pair of shoelaces, held ready in inventory against the fateful day that mine wore down and snapped. Disappointingly, the aisle labeled "footcare" offered only packets of corn cushions, corn files, corn/callus removers, toe cap/sleeves, ingrown-toenail relievers, and the rest of the Dr. Scholl's line. I checked "hosiery," but found only stockings. I was almost ready to believe that CVS didn't carry what I needed, when, turning down aisle 8A, marked "cleaners," I saw them,

[1] Already the disruption begins: the last few times I visited a CVS *they did not staple my bag at all,* though the stapler was lying right there by the cash register—they had switched to using a plastic bag with two integral carry-loops that made it look like the top of a pair of overalls, and this plastic was impossible to staple effectively. I wonder whether close observation and time-motion studies showed CVS management that because the stores were permanently understaffed, the higher incidence of successful shoplifting attendant on unsecured bags would be more than outweighed by the faster throughput of cashiers who did not have to spend extra seconds stapling.

hanging over cans of Kiwi shoe polish, next to sponges and flock-lined latex gloves. They were CVS's house brand, sixty-nine-cent "replacement dress laces." A slight cheapo glint led me to suspect that they were woven of man-made fibers; but at the shoelace level of detail, nobody could reasonably demand cotton. A chart on the back of each package correlated the number of paired eyelets in your shoes with the length of shoelace you needed: counting mine (five), I bought the twenty-seven-inch size. My shoes looked scuffed, and I almost bought a can of black Kiwi polish as well—I was attracted by the archaism of the canister's design: it was American, yet easily as good as the cans of Filippo Berio olive oil; and there was a nice resemblance between the kiwi bird standing in its white semicircle and the white, encircled Penguin on the black paperback I was carrying. But I remembered that I had several cans of Kiwi black at home—it was a wonder, really, that Kiwi made any money at all in this business, given how long each canister lasted, I thought: you lost it in the bottom of your closet long before you ran out.

There were lines at all the cash registers. I studied the technique of the cashiers and chose the smartest-looking one, an Indian or Pakistani woman in a blue sweater, even though her line was two people longer than any of the others, because I had come to the conclusion that the differential in checkout speeds between a fast, smart ringer-upper and a slow, dumb one was three transactions to one, such was the variation in human abilities and native intelligence—even four to one if there were sophisticated transactions like returns, or the appearance of something whose price had to be looked up in the alphabetical printout because it wasn't price-gunned on the package. This Indian woman was a true professional: she put the items in the bag as she rang them up, eliminating the need to handle everything twice, and she did not wait to see whether the customer had the exact change: she had learned that when the guy said, "Wait, I think I have it!" there was a good chance that after all his fishing and palm-counting, the combination of coins would prove to be inadequate, and he would say, "Sorry, I don't," and hand her a twenty-dollar bill. She closed the register drawer with her hips and tore the receipt off at almost precisely the same moment, and her use of the chrome handgrip-style stapler that was chained to the counter was everything you want to see in bag stapling. Her only difficulty came when, making change for the woman in front of me (tweezers, Vaseline Intensive Care, Trident gum, nude-colored stockings, and a package of Marlboro Light 100s), she ran out of loose dimes. The coin roll was made of thick shrink-wrapped plastic. It took her ten seconds of unvexed, expressionless bending and prying to work four dimes out into the coin trough.[1] Even with this setback, however, I reached her with my shoelaces faster than I would have reached any of the other cashiers. (To be truthful, I had watched her before, when I was at the store to buy earplugs, and thus I already knew that she was the fastest.) I broke a ten. She laid the bills on my palm and released the loose coins into the curve the bills formed—the riskiest, most skillful way, which left me with a hand free to take hold of the bag, and which avoided that sometimes embarrassing touch of a stranger's warm hand. I wanted to tell her how nimble she was, that I really liked the fact that she had discovered the movements and shortcuts that kept cash transactions enjoyable, but there didn't seem to be any unembarrassing way of conveying this. She smiled and nodded ceremonially, and I left, my errand complete.

[1] I forgave her completely for this delay: these plastic coin rolls were a very unhappy development in the life of the cashier. Paper coin rolls had beauty: interesting pulpy colors, soft paper-bag paper but heavy with the density of money inside; and good cashiers could crack them open against the edge of a coin trough and have their entire contents poured into place in five seconds. But even so, when I first saw the plastic rolls (around 1980), I was excited, I was upbeat: you could tell more easily from the edges of the ranked coins which they were, and the plastic was probably the product of some magnificent sorter/counter/packager/bundler at the bank. But plastic, unless it is made unmanageably thick, will, unlike paper, tear easily once it has been nicked (as in shrink-wrapping on record albums)—and nicks undoubtedly would happen in big heavy bags of coin rolls: thus the plastic coin roll advocates were evidently forced to adopt a thickness of their chosen material that made the cashier's life a time of periodic exasperation, especially if she had long fingernails. What we needed here was some kind of pull tab, extending the length of the roll, similar to the thread in the Band-Aid wrapper, except functional.

Chapter Fourteen

ON THE WAY BACK, my office seemed farther from the CVS than it had on the way there. I ate a vendor's hot dog with sauerkraut (a combination whose tastiness still makes me tremble), walking fast in order to save as much of the twenty minutes of my lunch hour I had left for reading. A cookie store I passed had no customers in it; in under thirty seconds, I had bought a large, flexible chocolate chip cookie there for eighty cents. Waiting for a light five blocks away from my building, I took a bite of the cookie; immediately I felt a strong need for some milk to complement it, and I nipped into a Papa Gino's and bought a half-pint carton in a bag. Thus supplied, full of thoughts about the ritual aspects of bagging, I returned to the brick plaza and sat down on a bench in the sun near the revolving door. It was a neo-Victorian bench, made of thin slats of wood bolted to curves of ornate iron and painted green—a kind that might be thought overly cute now, but which at that time seemed rare and wonderful, architects having then only recently begun to abandon the low, evil slabs of cast concrete or polished granite that had served as places to sit (or slump, for they offered no back support) in this sort of public area for twenty regressive years.

I placed the CVS bag beside me and opened the carton of milk, pushing an edge of the bag Donna had given me under my thigh so that it would not blow away. The bench gave me a three-quarter view of my building: the mezzanine floor, a grid of dark green glass with vertical marble accents, was the last wide story before the façade angled in and took off, neck-defyingly, into a squint of blue haze. The building's shadow had reached one end of my bench. It was a perfect day for fifteen minutes of reading. I opened the Penguin Classic at the placemarker (a cash-machine receipt, which I slipped for the time being several pages ahead), and then I took a bite of cookie and a mouthful of cold milk. Until my eyes adjusted, the pages were blinding, illegible hillocks, tinted with after-images of retinal violets and greens. I blinked and chewed. The independence of the bite of cookie and the mouthful of milk began to merge and warm pleasantly in my mouth; another pure infusion of milk coldly washed the sweet mash down.[1] I found my place on the brilliant page and read:

> Observe, in short, how transient and trivial is all mortal life; yesterday a drop of semen, tomorrow a handful of spice and ashes.

Wrong, wrong, wrong! I thought. Destructive and unhelpful and misguided and completely untrue!—but harmless, even

[1] My mother had said unexpectedly one afternoon while we both sat at the kitchen table (I was reading "Dear Abby" while finishing a peanut butter sandwich and a glass of milk; she was reading *Readings in the Philosophy of the Social Sciences* for a course she was taking) that it was not a good idea to take a drink of what you were drinking before you had swallowed what you were chewing—not, she explained when I asked her why, because you were more likely to choke, but because it was considered rude; rude in a subtler way, apparently, than the childish crudity of talking with your mouth full or "smacking your lips" (a phrase I still don't fully understand), because, though you offered no unpleasant sights or noises to others present, you did allow them to make undesirably detailed inferences about the squelchy mixing and churning that was going on behind your sealed lips. The thought that I had grossed my own mother out at the kitchen table was painful to me; I never again took a sip while still chewing in public, and I felt my stomach flip when others did; but since in the case of milk and cookies simultaneity really is the only way to deflect the killing sweetness of the cookie and camouflage the Pepto-Bismolian cheesiness of the milk, I went ahead, relatively unobserved there on the bench, and bit and sipped by turns.

agreeably sobering, to a man sitting on a green bench on a herringbone-patterned brick plaza near fifteen healthy, regularly spaced trees, within earshot of the rubbery groan and whish of a revolving door. I could absorb any brutal stoicism anyone dished out! Instead of continuing, however, I took another bite of cookie and mouthful of milk. That was the problem with reading: you always had to pick up again at the very thing that had made you stop reading the day before. A glowing mention in William Edward Hartpole Lecky's *History of European Morals* (which I had been attracted to, browsing in the library one Saturday, by the ambitious title and the luxuriant incidentalism of the footnotes[1]) was what had made me stop in front of the floor-to-ceiling shelf of Penguin Classics at

[1] In one footnote, for instance, Lecky quotes a French biographer of Spinoza to the effect that the philosopher liked to entertain himself by dropping flies into spiders' webs, enjoying the resultant battle so much that he occasionally burst out laughing. (*History of European Morals,* vol. 1, page 289.) Lecky uses this tidbit to illustrate his contention that sophisticated moral feelings are not consistent across a personality or a culture; you can be eloquently virtuous in one sphere, while tolerant of nastiness, or even nasty yourself, in another—a familiar enough point, perhaps, but never pivoting on the example of Spinoza before, I don't think. Hobbes, too, we learn in a Penguin selection of John Aubrey's *Lives,* page 228, liked during college ("rook racked" Oxford) to get up early in the morning and trap jackdaws with sticky string, using cheese as bait, hauling them in, fluttering and wrapped in the feather-destroying snare, apparently for fun. Jesus H. Christ! As our knowledge of these philosophers is brought within this domestic and anecdotal embrace, we can't help having our estimation of them somewhat diminished by these cruel, small pursuits. And Wittgenstein, as well, I read in some biography, loved to watch cowboy movies: he would go every afternoon to watch gunfights and arrows through the chest for hours at a time. Can you take seriously a person's theory of language when you know that he was delighted by the woodenness and tedium of cowboy movies? Once in a while, fine—but every day? Yet while these tiny truths about three philosophers (of whom, to be honest, I have read very little) have at least temporarily disabled any interest I might have had in reading them further, I crave knowledge of this kind of detail. As Boswell said, "Upon this tour, when journeying, he [Johnson] wore boots, and a very wide brown cloth great coat, with pockets which might have almost held the two volumes of his folio dictionary; and he carried in his hand a large English oak stick. Let me not be censured for mentioning such minute particulars. Everything relative to so great a man is worth observing. I remember Dr Adam Smith, in his rhetorical lectures at Glascow, told us he was glad to know that Milton wore latchets in his shoes, instead of buckles." (Boswell, *Journal of a Tour to the Hebrides,* Penguin, page 165. Think of it: *John Milton wore shoelaces!*) Boswell, like Lecky (to get back to the point of this footnote), and Gibbon

the bookstore on a lunch hour two weeks earlier and reach for the thin volume of Aurelius's *Meditations* on the very top shelf, disdaining the footstool that was available, hooking my finger on the top of the book and pulling it so that it half fell into my palm: a thinner Penguin than most, glossy, inflexible, mint-condition. In earlier short-lived classical enthusiasms I had bought, and read no more than twenty pages of, Penguin

---

before him, loved footnotes. They knew that the outer surface of truth is not smooth, welling and gathering from paragraph to shapely paragraph, but is encrusted with a rough protective bark of citations, quotation marks, italics, and foreign languages, a whole variorum crust of "ibid.'s" and "compare's" and "see's" that are the shield for the pure flow of argument as it lives for a moment in one mind. They knew the anticipatory pleasure of sensing with peripheral vision, as they turned the page, a gray silt of further example and qualification waiting in tiny type at the bottom. (They were aware, more generally, of the usefulness of tiny type in enhancing the glee of reading works of obscure scholarship: typographical density forces you to crouch like Robert Hooke or Henry Gray over the busyness and intricacy of recorded truth.) They liked deciding as they read whether they would bother to consult a certain footnote or not, and whether they would read it in context, or read it before the text it hung from, as an hors d'oeuvre. The muscles of the eye, they knew, want vertical itineraries; the rectus externus and internus grow dazed waggling back and forth in the Zs taught in grade school: the footnote functions as a switch, offering the model-railroader's satisfaction of catching the march of thought with a superscripted "1" and routing it, sometimes at length, through abandoned stations and submerged, leaching tunnels. Digression—a movement away from the *gradus*, or upward escalation, of the argument—is sometimes the only way to be thorough, and footnotes are the only form of graphic digression sanctioned by centuries of typesetters. And yet the MLA Style Sheet I owned in college warned against lengthy, "essay-like" footnotes. Were they *nuts*? Where is scholarship *going*? (They have removed this blemish in later editions.) It is true that Johnson said, on the subject of exegetical notes to Shakespeare, "The mind is refrigerated by interruption; the thoughts are diverted from the principal subject; the reader is weary, he suspects not why; and at last throws away the book, which he has too diligently studied." ("Preface to Shakespeare.") But Johnson was referring here to the special case of one writer's commentary on another—and indeed whose mind is not chilled by several degrees when the editors of the *Norton Anthology of Poetry* clarify every potentially confusing word or line for us, failing to understand that the student's pleasure in poetry comes in part from the upper furze of nouns he can't quite place and allusions that he only half recognizes? Do we really need Tennyson's "unnumbered and enormous polypi" neatly footnoted with "3. Octopus-like creatures"? Do we need the very title of that poem ("The Kraken," printed on pages 338–339 of the revised shorter edition of that anthology) explained away for us? And do we need the *opening sentence* of James's *The American*, which mentions the "Salon Carré, in the Museum

Classics of Arrian, Tacitus, Cicero, and Procopius—I liked to see them lined up on my windowsill, just above the shelf that held my records; I liked them in part because, having come to history first through the backs of record albums, I associated the Classics' blackness and gloss with record vinyl.[1] Lecky had praised Aurelius in a way that made reading him seem irresistible:

> Tried by the chequered events of a reign of nineteen years, presiding over a society that was profoundly corrupt, and over a city that was notorious for its license, the perfection of his character awed even calumny to silence, and the spontaneous sentiment of his people proclaimed him rather a god than a man. Very few men have ever lived concerning whose inner life we can speak so confidently. His *Meditations*, which form one of the most impressive, form also one of the truest, books in the whole range of religious literature.

And sure enough, the first thing I read when I opened the *Meditations* at random in the bookstore stunned me with its

---

of the Louvre," dental-flossed (in the Penguin American Library edition, of all places) with the following demoralizing aid:

> 1. The heart of the picture-galleries in the great French national museum, this room contains, in addition to works by the old masters whom James mentions below, Leonardo's "Mona Lisa."

But the great scholarly or anecdotal footnotes of Lecky, Gibbon, or Boswell, written by the author of the book himself to supplement, or even correct over several later editions, what he says in the primary text, are reassurances that the pursuit of truth doesn't have clear outer boundaries: it doesn't end with the book; restatement and self-disagreement and the enveloping sea of referenced authorities all continue. Footnotes are the finer-suckered surfaces that allow tentacular paragraphs to hold fast to the wider reality of the library.

[1] I also liked the black Penguins because on the front page they had a biographical note about the translator that was in the same small print as the biographical note about the major historical figure he had rendered into English, a pairing that made those minor translational lives in Dorset and Leeds seem just as important as the often assassinating, catty, and conspiring lives of the ancients. The Penguin translators seemed frequently to be amateurs, not academics, who had, after getting their double firsts, lived quietly running their fathers' businesses or being clergymen, and translating in the evenings—probably gay, a fair number of them: that excellent low-key sort of man who achieves little by external standards but who sustains civilization for us by knowing, in a perfectly balanced, accessible, and considered way, all that can be known about several brief periods of Dutch history, or about the flowering of some especially rich tradition of terra-cotta pipes.

fineness. "Manifestly," I read (the warped sound of a rinsed saucepan struck against the side of the sink ringing in my head),

> Manifestly, no condition of life could be so well adapted for the practice of philosophy as this in which chance finds you today!

Wo! I loved the slight awkwardness and archaism of the sentence, full of phrases that never come naturally to people's lips now but once had: "condition of life," "so well adapted for," "chance finds you," as well as the unexpected but apt rush to an exclamation point at the end. But mainly I thought that the statement was extraordinarily true and that if I bought that book and learned how to act upon that single sentence I would be led into elaborate realms of understanding, even as I continued to do, outwardly, exactly as I had done, going to work, going to lunch, going home, talking to L. on the phone or having her over for the night. As often happens, I liked that first deciding sentence better than anything I came across in later consecutive reading. I had been carrying the book around for two weeks of lunch hours; its spine was worn from being held more than from being read, although a single white foldline did run down the back, which made the book open automatically to page 168, where the "condition of life" sentence was; and by now, disenchanted, flipping around a lot, I was nearly ready to abandon it entirely, tired of Aurelius's unrelenting and morbid self-denial. This latest thing about mortal life's being no more than sperm and ash, read two days in a row, was too much for me. I replaced the cash-machine receipt in the page, where it remained until quite recently, and I closed the book.

Half the milk remained to be drunk. Feeling now won back by the taste, I downed it all at once; and then, remembering a habit of childhood, I balled up the cookie bag, which was made of a thin, crinkly kind of paper, and stuffed it into the spout of the milk carton. Ten minutes of lunch hour remained. If I wasn't going to read, I felt that I should spend the time replacing my worn-out shoelaces with the ones I had just bought. But the sun was too warm for that: inclining my face toward it, I sat with my eyes closed, my arms outstretched on the bench, and my legs crossed at the ankles in front of me, drawing in my feet whenever I heard a person walking nearby, in case I was blocking the way. My right hand, in the shade, touched the cool dome of a neo-Victorian bolt; my left hand, in the sun, touched hot, smooth, green paint; a current of complete peaceful contentment began to flow from the shade hand to the sun hand, passing through my arms and shoulders and whorling up into my brain along the way. "Manifestly," I repeated, as if scolding myself, "no condition of life could be so well adapted for the practice of philosophy as this in which chance finds you today!" Chance found me that day having worked for a living all morning, broken a shoelace, chatted with Tina, urinated successfully in a corporate setting, washed my face, eaten half of a bag of popcorn, bought a new set of shoelaces, eaten a hot dog and a cookie with some milk; and chance found me now sitting in the sun on a green bench, with a paperback on my lap. What, philosophically, was I supposed to do with that? I looked down at the book. A gold bust of the emperor was on the cover. Who bought this kind of book? I wondered. People like me, sporadic self-improvers, on lunch hours? Or only students? Or cabbies, wanting something to surprise their fares with, a book to wave in front of the Plexiglas? I had often wondered whether Penguin made money selling these paperbacks.

And then I considered the phrase "often wondered." Feeling Aurelius pressing me to practice philosophy on the scant raw materials of my life, I asked myself exactly *how often* I had wondered about the profitability of Penguin Classics. Merely saying that you often wondered something gave no indication of how prominent a part of life that state of mind really was. Did it come up every three hours? Once a month? Every time a certain special set of conditions recurred to remind me? I certainly did not think about Penguin's financial condition every time I set eyes on one of their books. Sometimes I just thought of whatever that particular book was about, uninterested for the moment in who the publisher was; sometimes I thought of the fact that the orange-backed Penguin novels faded in the sunlight like dry cleaners' posters, and how amazing it was that a color scheme as intrinsically questionable as that orange, white, and black would come to seem lovely and subtle, intimately associated with our idea of the English novel, just because it happened to be what somebody at a publishing firm had decided to use as a standard format. Sometimes the orange backs made me think of the first Penguin book I had read, *My Family and Other Animals:* my mother had given it to me one summer, and not only had I liked the lizards and scorpions and sunlight, I had also been interested, as I read my way deeper into the bulk of the pages, by a tiny printed code that occurred every twenty pages or so at the bottom left margin of the right-hand page: "FOA-7," "FOA-8," "FOA-9," etc. Some kind of private technical bookbinder's jargon, I thought—"Facing Off Alternate 7," or "Feed Onto Assembly 7," perhaps. Much later, when I noticed this feature of Penguin books again, in the middle of reading Iris Murdoch's *A Fairly Honourable Defeat* ("F.H.D.-6," etc.) and realized that it was simply the initials of the book's title, a quick way of avoiding mixups in manufacture, I felt a retroactive reach of love for this previously unsolved mystery, and gratitude to Penguin for providing us with this more absolute set of milestones to measure our progress through a book: for when you reach something like "F.H.D.-14" (as far as I got in that particular Murdoch, I have to say, much as I like her writing), you feel that your forward progress is confirmed more objectively than when you merely reach a new chapter.

All of these particular Penguin-related observations had different cycles of recurrence and therefore microscopic differences of weight in my personality—and it seemed to me then that we needed a measure of the *periodicity* of regularly returning thoughts, expressed as, say, the number of times a certain thought pops into your head every year. I wondered about the financial situation of Penguin books maybe four times a year. "A periodicity of 4"—it had a scientific ring. Once a year, just when Muzak switched over to Christmas carols, I thought, "It's funny that 'God Rest Ye Merry, Gentlemen' is in a minor key." Every time I stubbed a toe I thought, "Amazing that a man's toe can take that kind of shock and not break"—and I stubbed a toe maybe eight times a year. About every other time I took a vitamin C pill, fifteen times a year, I thought as I filled the water glass, ". . . livin' on reds, vitamin C, and cocaine . . ." If we could assign a periodicity number in this way to every recurrent thought a person had, what would we know? We would know the relative frequency of his thoughts over time, something that might prove to be more revealing than any statement of beliefs he might offer, or even than a frozen section of available, potential thoughts (if that were possible) at any one time in particular. Just as the most frequent words in English are humdrum ones like "of" and "in" and "the," so the most frequent thoughts are bland and tiresome things like, "Itch on face," "[fleeting sexual image]," and "Is my breath bad?" But below the "of" and "in" level of thought-vocabulary, there was a whole list of mid-frequency ideas. I imagined them taking the form of a chart—something like:

Subject of Thought	*Number of Times Thought Occurred per Year (in descending order)*
L.	580.0
Family	400.0
Brushing tongue	150.0
Earplugs	100.0
Bill-paying	52.0
Panasonic three-wheeled vacuum cleaner, greatness of	45.0
Sunlight makes you cheerful	40.0
Traffic frustration	38.0
Penguin books, all	35.0
Job, should I quit?	34.0
Friends, don't have any	33.0
Marriage, a possibility?	32.0
Vending machines	31.0
Straws don't unsheath well	28.0
Shine on moving objects	25.0
McCartney more talented than Lennon?	23.0
Friends smarter, more capable than I am	19.0
Paper-towel dispensers	19.0
"What oft was thought, but ne'er" etc.	18.0
People are very dissimilar	16.0
Trees, beauty of	15.0
Sidewalks	15.0
Friends are unworthy of me	15.0
Identical twins separated at birth, studies of traits	14.0

Subject of Thought	*Number of Times Thought Occurred per Year (in descending order)*
Intelligence, going fast	14.0
Wheelchair ramps, their insane danger	14.0
Urge to kill	13.0
Escalator invention	12.0
People are very similar	12.0
"Not in my backyard"	11.0
Straws float now	10.0
DJ, would I be happy as one?	9.0
"If you can't get out of it, get into it"	9.0
Pen, felt-tip	9.0
Gasoline, nice smell of	8.0
Pen, ballpoint	8.0
Stereo systems	8.0
Fear of getting mugged again	7.0
Staplers	7.0
"Roaches check in, but they don't check out"	6.0
Dinner roll, image of	6.0
Shoes	6.0
Bags	5.0
Butz, Earl	4.0
Sweeping, brooms	4.0
Whistling, yodel trick	4.0
"You can taste it with your eyes"	4.0
Dry-cleaning fluid, smell of	3.0
Zip-lock tops	2.0
Popcorn	1.0
Birds regurgitate food and feed young with it	0.5
Kant, Immanuel	0.5

But compiling the list, as I saw as soon as I began sketchily to do so in my head, was not the enlightening process of abstraction I had expected it to be: thoughts were too fluid, too difficult to name, and once named to classify, for my estimate of their relative frequency to mean very much. And there were way, way too many of them. Yet this ranking of periodicity, as an ideal of description, was the best I could do that afternoon. Introspection was the only slightly philosophical activity I felt capable of practicing, sitting on the bench in the sun, waiting until the last possible minute before I went back into work; and the attribution of frequency did at least force a truer sort of introspection than the wide-open question "What do I think about?" People seemed so alike when you imagined their daily schedules, or watched them walk toward the revolving door (as Dave, Sue, and Steve, not noticing me, were doing now), yet if you imagined a detailed thought-frequency chart compiled for each of them, and you tried comparing one chart with another, you would feel suddenly as if you were comparing beings as different from each other as an extension cord and a grape-leaf roll. L. once told me that she thought "all the time" (I asked her to be more specific, she said once every three weeks or so) about a disturbing joke someone had told her when she was eleven, which goes: "Q: Do you know the description of the perfect woman? A: [Puts hand waist-high.] This tall with a flat head to rest your beer on." Until two or three years ago, she told me, she had, from the time she was ten or so, often against her will, thought several times a week of a rhymed riddle that went:

> As I was walking to St. Ives
> I met a man with seven wives
> Every wife held seven sacks
> And every sack held seven cats
> And every cat had seven kits
> Kits cats sacks wives
> How many were going to St. Ives?

Every month and a half, so she told me, she thought with pleasure of a description in *Daniel Deronda* of a room in which everything was yellow, not having imagined high-Victorian rooms decorated in that color before. And I thought about none of those things![1] She and I knew each other well; we felt

[1] Not quite true anymore. Since she told me the St. Ives riddle, it has taken a place on my carousel, too: I'm bothered that the answer is supposed to be "None, dummy—the man was coming *from* St. Ives," because (a) you can certainly "meet" a person on the road by falling in step with him and talking to him; and (b) the line is not specific as to whether the man has seven wives "with" him right there on the road, or merely that he is responsible for seven wives as an ongoing condition of his life. I worry, thus, about how much perplexity a riddle like this would have caused children in households where riddles were exchanged; whether I would have liked this perplexity as a

that we were alike in important ways, delighted and not delighted in tandem, yet charts of repeating thoughts and their periodicities for the two of us would reveal surprisingly little overlap in the mid-frequency range.

Above the periodicity of solitary, internal thought, dependent upon it yet existing on a separate plane, was the periodicity of conversation, on the phone and in person. Twenty times a year L. and I talked about the fact that women characters in film comedies almost always functioned as comic straight men. Twenty-five times a year we wondered what it would have been like if my parents had stayed married, or if hers had gotten a divorce. Fifty times a year we talked about promiscuity's effects on outlook and personality, with examples taken from her friends' lives and from our own. Every other day we considered which city or area we would most like to live in, and in what kind of house, if we were rich. Affirmative action had a periodicity of 4; the heritability of mental traits, of 12. Twice every summer we discussed whether colors in nature could clash. When a subject recurred, we felt it as familiar, but indistinct: almost always it came up (that is, felt worth discussing again) only after we could no longer remember exactly what our previous respective opinions had been—we remembered vaguely, unattributively, the telling points that had been made the last time, but often reversed our positions, each of us more enthusiastic now about the fresher-feeling arguments the other had made the last time, and less convinced by our own earlier ones.

And there were periodicities superimposed on the plane of conversation, too: nationwide fifteen-year cycles of journalistic excitement about one issue or another; generational corrections and pendular overreactions; and, above these, the periodicity of libraries and Penguin Classics, slower still, resurgencies and subsidings of interest in some avenue of inquiry or style of thinking from one century to the next, restatings of mislaid truths in new vernaculars.

---

child if I had been exposed to it (rather than to, say, Jack and Spot and their wagon); what the intention of the original framer of the riddle had been; and what station in life he or she had occupied—I think about it all roughly nineteen times a year.

On all these planes, I thought, the alternation of neglect and attention paid to an idea was like the cycle of waxing and buffing, dulling down and raising the shine higher, sanding between coats and then applying another—things happened to it during the long unsupervised stretches. Just now, for the sixth time in two workweeks, I had paid attention to one sentence-long idea of Aurelius for a minute or two, thereby lifting it up from artificial Penguin storage into living memory for that short time, when but for its occupying my thoughts, it might not have been for those minutes under consideration by anyone else in the entire city, maybe even in the world. Today, too, for the first time in twenty years, I had on two separate occasions been reminded of the act of tying my shoelaces (three occasions, if you count the momentary pride I had felt just before the shoelace had snapped), a lifetime average periodicity of around one-tenth of a reminding per year, although that number is misleading, since frequencies should, I decided, be averaged over a shorter interval, like five years, to be meaningful, at least until you have died. It was impossible to predict which of the two, Aurelius or shoelaces, would rank higher in my overall lifetime periodicity ratings upon my death.[1]

[1] I am fairly certain now that shoelaces will rank higher. In the course of preparing the present record of that Aurelius-and-shoelace noon, I lived through a rigorous month in which the subject of shoelace-tying and shoelace wear came up 325 times, whereas Aurelius's sentiment cycled around only 90 times. I doubt very much that I will ever concentrate on either of them again, having worn both of the thoughts out for myself. But these sudden later flurries may not count, since they are artificial duplicative retrievals performed in order to understand how the earlier natural retrievals had come about. The very last instance of shoelace thought happened as follows: by chance, I was flipping through the 1984–1986 *Research Reports* of MIT's Laboratory for Manufacturing and Productivity at my office, and I noticed that there was active work going forward on the subject of the "pathology of worn ropes." The research was described as follows:

> Numerous marine ropes have been gathered from around the world, representing a variety of deployment modes and periods of exposure Patterns of mechanical and chemical deterioration were detected and quantified. Major mechanisms of deterioration have been established for specific deployments. Degradation patterns are now being assembled for application to structural models of ropes with a view towards establishing a valid retirement policy.

Degradation patterns were now being assembled! Iyiyi! Aside from deciding, very briefly, that I had to quit my job and apprentice myself to this exciting project, I wondered whether S. Backer and M. Seo's results could be adapted

...e to go in. The fingers of my sun hand felt sticky; I ... them with my thumb until a tiny dark-gray cylinder, ...posed of popcorn oil, urban dirt, skin, and cookie sugar, was brought into being. I flicked it away. The date, I noticed, was still visible on my palm, but it would be gone after my next hand-washing. With some effort I was able to twist and crumple the Papa Gino's bag tightly enough to stuff most of it, too, into the milk carton; I took an obscure satisfaction in the

---

so that they applied, however crudely, to the case of my own shoelaces. To my surprise, the library did not own a copy of the referenced September 1985 *Proceedings of the Third Japan-Australia Joint Symposium on Objective Measurement: Application to Product Design and Process Control.* I wrote for a reprint, but in the meantime my impatience drove me to look further. I soon found that I had been a fool to think that the twisted pathology of marine ropes could have had anything to do with the woven pathology of shoelaces. I consulted volume 07.01 of the massive guidelines of the American Society for Testing and Materials, and found a discussion of the procedures and instrumentation for the abrasional testing of textiles. The abrasion machines pictured looked like they were products of the 1930s, but in the realm of abrasion, the known effect of established testing machines might, I thought, be more important than sophisticated instrumentation. This also proved to be untrue. Moving to the periodical literature, I learned of the Microcon I, the Instron Tensile Tester, the Accelerator Abrasion Tester, and the Stoll Quarter Master Universal Wear Tester, or SQMUWT. (For this last, see *Textile Technology Digest,* 05153/80; Pal, Munshi, and Ukidre, of India's Cotton Technology Research Laboratory, have used the machine in the determination of flex abrasion of sewing threads.) Nonetheless, as H. M. Elder, T. S. Ellis, and F. Yahya of the Fibre and Textile Unit, Department of Pure and Applied Chemistry, University of Strathclyde, Glasgow, write, "it is doubtful if any one machine can be developed that is able to duplicate the complex range of abrasive stresses, and their respective proportions, to which a textile material is subjected in service." (*J. Text. Inst.,* 1987, No. 2, p. 72.) This Scottish skepticism was exhilarating, since it bore out what I had myself suspected in those first few minutes in my office, after my second pair of shoelaces had snapped.

And then, checking the 1984 volumes of *World Textile Abstracts,* I read entry 4522:

> **Methods for evaluating the abrasion resistance and knot slippage strength of shoe laces**
>
> Z. Czaplicki
>
> *Technik Wlokienniczy,* 1984, **33** No.1, 3-4 (2 pages). In Polish.
>
> Two mechanical devices for testing the abrasion resistance and knot slippage performance of shoe laces are described and investigated. Polish standards are discussed. [C] **1984/4522**

I let out a small cry and slapped my hand down on the page. The joy I felt may be difficult for some to understand. Here was a man, Z. Czaplicki, who *had to know!* He was not going to abandon the problem with some sigh about

inside-outness of this achievement. Collecting my possessions, my stapled CVS bag and my paperback, I stood up. The stuffed carton of milk I threw out; or, more accurately, I placed it very carefully at the apex of a mound of bee-probed lunch trash ready at any minute to overflow a nearby oil drum, making sure the carton wasn't going to topple at least until I was gone by steadying it gently with my fingertips in its precarious spot for a few seconds. I couldn't crush the underlying trash down, as I had half an hour earlier outside the CVS, because any application of pressure would only have made the whole mound disintegrate. A bee rose up from a sun-filled paper cup, off to make slum honey from some diet root beer it had found inside. I entered the lobby and made my way toward the up escalator.

---

complexity and human limitation after a minute's thought, as I had, and go to lunch—*he was going to make the problem his life's work*. Don't tell me he received a centralized directive to look into a more durable weave of shoelace for the export market. Oh no! His very own shoelace had snapped one time too many one morning, and instead of buying a pair of replacement dress laces at the corner *farmacja* and forgetting about the problem until the next time, he had constructed a machine and strapped hundreds of shoelaces of all kinds into it, wearing them down over and over, in a passionate effort to get some subtler idea of the forces at work. And he had gone beyond that—he had built another machine to determine which surface texture of shoelace would best hold its knot, so that humanity would not have to keep retying its shoelaces all day long and wearing them out before their time. A great man! I left the library relieved. Progress was being made. Someone was looking into the problem. Mr. Czaplicki, in Poland, would take it from there.

Chapter Fifteen

AT THE VERY END of the ride, I caught sight of a cigarette butt rolling and hopping against the comb plate where the grooves disappeared. I stepped onto the mezzanine and turned to watch it for a few seconds. Its movement was a faster version of the rotation of mayonnaise or peanut butter or olive jars, or cans of orange juice or soup, when they are caught at the end of supermarket conveyor belts, their labels circling around and around—Hellman's! Hellman's! Hellman's!—something I had loved to see when I was little. I looked down the great silver glacier to the lobby. The maintenance man was at the bottom. I waved to him. He held up his white rag for a second, then put it back down on the rubber handrail.

For further information about Granta Books
and a full list of titles, please write to us at

Granta Books

2/3 HANOVER YARD

NOEL ROAD

LONDON

N1 8BE

enclosing a stamped, addressed envelope

You can visit our website at

http://www.granta.com